TOO-CLOSE SHAVE

Skye saw the arrow hurtling straight at him.
He ducked, flattening himself across the
Ovaro's neck as the shaft grazed his back.
He saw the Indian charging straight at
him, his pony galloping full-out.

Fargo tried to use his big Sharps, but had
time only to swing the rifle stock upward
to parry a vicious swing of a tomahawk. The
blow sent Fargo spinning off his horse.

THE
TRAILSMAN

112

THE
DOOMSDAY
WAGONS

by

Jon Sharpe

A SIGNET BOOK

SIGNET
Published by the Penguin Group
Penguin Books USA Inc., 375 Hudson Street,
New York, New York 10014, U.S.A.
Penguin Books Ltd, 27 Wrights Lane,
London W8 5TZ, England
Penguin Books Australia Ltd, Ringwood,
Victoria, Australia
Penguin Books Canada Ltd, 2801 John Street,
Markham, Ontario, Canada L3R 1B4
Penguin Books (N.Z.) Ltd, 182-190 Wairau Road,
Auckland 10, New Zealand

Penguin Books Ltd, Registered Offices:
Harmondsworth, Middlesex, England

First published by Signet, an imprint of New American Library,
a division of Penguin Books USA Inc.

First Printing, April, 1991

10 9 8 7 6 5 4 3 2 1

The first chapter of this book previously appeared in *Blood Canyon*, the one
hundred eleventh volume in this series.

PUBLISHER'S NOTE
This is a work of fiction. Names, characters, places, and incidents either
are the product of the author's imagination or are used fictitiously, and any
resemblance to actual persons, living or dead, events, or locales is entirely
coincidental.

BOOKS ARE AVAILABLE AT QUANTITY DISCOUNTS WHEN USED TO PROMOTE
PRODUCTS OR SERVICES. FOR INFORMATION PLEASE WRITE TO PREMIUM MAR-
KETING DIVISION, PENGUIN BOOKS USA INC., 375 HUDSON STREET, NEW YORK,
NEW YORK 10014.

The Trailsman

Beginnings . . . they bend the tree and they mark the man. Skye Fargo was born when he was eighteen. Terror was his midwife, vengeance his first cry. Killing spawned Skye Fargo, ruthless, cold-blooded murder. Out of the acrid smoke of gunpowder still hanging in the air, he rose, cried out a promise never forgotten.

The Trailsman they began to call him all across the West: searcher, scout, hunter, the man who could see where others only looked, his skills for hire but not his soul, the man who lived each day to the fullest, yet trailed each tomorrow. Skye Fargo, the Trailsman, the seeker who could take the wildness of a land and the wanting of a woman and make them his own.

*They took the red man's name
for the land and he wrote his claim
in blood. Minnesota, 1860, the north country . . .*

1

The big man's lake-blue eyes narrowed as he guided the magnificent black-and-white Ovaro through the mountain ash. He peered through the flat clusters of small white flowers to where the lone wagon rolled along the flat land below the high ridge: one wagon, a two-horse brace, and as far as he could see, a lone driver. Again he caught the flash of full, thick hair, yellow bright even in the gray, clouded afternoon. He could see a long-skirted brown dress but not much else as the woman leaned from one side of the wagon. She seemed to be studying the ground as she drove.

The big man's eyes lifted to peer a few hundred yards ahead of where he rode. The four half-naked, bronzed forms were still there, paralleling the wagon below on their sturdy, short-legged ponies. They had watched the lone wagon below for almost two hours, just as he had. The big man's lips edged a tight smile. He knew exactly what they were thinking. It was almost built into the Indian attitude, regardless of the tribe. He brought his gaze back to the wagon below, a big Owensboro mountain wagon fitted with top bows and a canvas top. No Conestoga but serviceable enough for a long hard trip.

A bitter sound came from his lips. Alone out here, she might have a hard trip, but it wouldn't be a long one. Maybe she had a good reason, the big man reckoned, though he couldn't think of one that didn't add up to monumental stupidity. A long breath escaped him, drawn from deep down in his powerful chest. He wanted to ride away. He couldn't go risking his neck to play Good Samaritan for every damn fool in the West. But he wouldn't ride away, he swore softly. Logic and reason were no match for conscience.

He'd go down to her. He'd give her a chance to survive, at least another day. His eyes went to the four horsemen who moved with ghostlike silence through the mountain ash. They'd see him when he moved down to her, of course, but there was no other way. Maybe it would be enough to make them move on. Maybe . . .

He pulled his lips back in a grimace as he turned the Ovaro up onto a higher ridge of thick tree cover. He put the horse into a trot and passed the four Indians on the ridge below. He continued on for another few hundred yards before he sent the Ovaro downward. The tree cover was heavy and he was far enough ahead. The four braves wouldn't see him until he emerged in the open down on the flat land.

Riding straight down, brushing against the smooth gray-brown bark of the ash as the wooded ridge grew more dense, he emerged onto the flat land at the bottom just as he saw the wagon come over a slight rise. He moved toward it, reined up directly in her path, and saw her bring the wagon to a halt some twenty-five yards from him. He slowly walked the Ovaro forward.

She was young, he saw, and at close range the yellow hair was flaxen, loose, and shoulder-length. He took in a strong but very attractive face, classical in its lines, well-defined cheekbones, a straight, thin nose. Eyebrows only a shade darker than the flaxen of her hair were thin arches over robin's-egg-blue eyes. Her lips were a little thin but perhaps because of the way she was holding them. The brown dress rested against a slender figure with a nice swell of breasts under the square neckline.

He saw her hand move to the seat beside her and come up with a long-barreled .54-caliber army rifle. "That's close enough, mister," she said, and Fargo halted. The rifle barrel was rock-steady, he saw, and he smiled.

"You'll not be needing that for me," he said.

"It stays," she said evenly.

"Taking no chances. Very smart," he said.

"Thank you," she returned coolly.

"Except it makes me wonder."

"Wonder what?"

"What the hell you're doing out here all by yourself like a goddamn fool."

Her robin's-egg-blue eyes flared. "That's my business," she snapped. "What do you want, mister?"

"Name's Fargo. Skye Fargo," the big man said calmly. "You've got yourself some company."

"I can see that," she sniffed.

"Not just me, honey. Four braves up on the ridge line. They've been riding along with you for the past two hours," Fargo said. Her eyes shot up to the thick tree cover on the ridges, scanned the scene for a long minute before turning back to him. "You won't see them. Not until they want you to," he said.

"But they're up there."

"That's right."

"For the past two hours."

"Just about."

"That means you've been riding along all that time, too."

"Right again," he said.

He saw her eyes study him for a moment. "Then

why haven't they come after me?" she questioned, more condescension than concern in her tone.

"Indians are real careful. One thing they hate above all else is being ambushed. It hits at their prowess as warriors," Fargo said. "But they're not only careful, they're logical."

"Meaning what exactly?" She frowned.

"They can't believe anybody would be so god-damn stupid as to come out here all by themselves," he said, and saw blue sparks in her eyes. "So they've been waiting and watching to make sure you're not the bait to sucker them into a trap. Soon as they're convinced you're not, they'll pounce on you quicker than a red-tailed hawk on a gopher."

The young woman's eyes moved up to sweep the thick trees on the ridge lines again, narrowed as they searched for any sign of movement. Finally they returned to the big man in front of her. "And you've come to help me," she said.

"That's the general idea," he said, and saw the skepticism in her eyes as she stared back. "You don't believe me, do you?" Fargo said.

"My mother told me always be careful of strangers who want to do you favors," she said.

"Sometimes a mother's advice is good. Sometimes it's not worth shit. This is one of those times," Fargo said, and felt himself growing impatient.

"Why don't you ride along ahead of me, about where you are, for the next few miles?" she said. "If they attack, you'll be here to help."

His smile was made of ice. "I'll be a sitting duck, the first one they'll take out. No, thanks, honey."

"You want to be in the wagon with me," she said.

"Or next to it," he replied.

"Sorry, I'll have to pass on that," she said firmly, and he realized he couldn't blame her. She was

12

alone, wary, and not about to swallow a stranger's story about being watched by Indians. It was simply the wrong time for her rightful skepticism and the rifle barrel's unwavering steadiness told him he'd not be convincing her any further. Her words echoed his thoughts. "Now, I'll be moving on and I suggest you go your way, Mr. Fargo," she said. "And I thank you for your concern."

"Good manners and good looks. Very nice," Fargo said.

"You forget about the goddamn-fool part?" she tossed back.

"No. That still goes," he said cheerfully, and paused to watch the robin's-egg-blue eyes flash before turning the Ovaro away. He felt her eyes watching him as he moved into the trees to disappear from her sight. He paused, glanced back, and saw her roll on, and he rode up toward the ridges. She wasn't the only one who had watched him leave, he knew, and he climbed the steep hillside to the first ridge and moved east through the trees. He rode with relaxed casualness, but all his wild-creature senses were tuned to the trees at his back. It took only a few minutes for him to pick up the horse and rider following through the mountain ash.

They were being completely predictable. They were probably Chippewa, he figured. He had expected they'd send one of their band to see where he went, and Fargo kept the Ovaro at a walk eastward along the ridge. The Indian hung back and would have been invisible to most men. The other three would do nothing till he returned, Fargo knew, and he had gone perhaps half a mile when he became aware that he was alone. His follower had left, convinced he was nothing more than a passing rider.

Fargo swung the Ovaro in a wide circle and

headed back the way he had come, taking care to stay back far enough not to be seen, heard, or smelled.

He kept glancing downward through the trees, but the wagon was still not in sight. It wasn't for another quarter-mile that he saw the four bronzed riders below, moving downward from the ridge. He glimpsed the wagon ahead, then, and saw one of the Indians spur his pony forward, still in the trees but almost at bottom of the hillside.

Fargo slowed and saw the other three move on until they were abreast of the wagon. It was then that he caught sight of the fourth Indian as the man emerged from the trees a dozen yards in front of the wagon.

The other three braves were suddenly moving fast, heading for the flat ground almost abreast of the wagon.

Fargo spurred the Ovaro forward. He saw the young woman bring the rifle up as the one Indian blocked her path. He watched her draw a bead on the Indian, rifle to her shoulder, waiting. It was only when the Indian suddenly sent his pony charging forward that she fired. But the brave was ready for the rifle shot and he flattened himself across the pony's neck. The shot went harmlessly over his back.

The young woman tried to get off another shot when two arrows grazed her shoulders from the right side of the wagon. she half-turned and ducked as another two shafts slammed through the canvas of the wagon. She tried to bring the rifle up to fire again, but the Indian had reached her from the front and with lithe grace he dived from his pony and sent her flying backward on the seat. The rifle fired into the air and he tore it from her grasp.

The other three braves had halted alongside the wagon and one started to climb from his pony onto the driver's seat of the big Owensboro. Fargo reached the edge of the trees and pulled the big Sharps from its saddle case. The rifle was at his shoulder as he skidded the Ovaro to a halt. He fired, and one of the Indians on the wagon did a backward somersault as he flew from the driver's seat in a shower of red. The two still on their ponies alongside the wagon whirled and one flew backward from his pony as if on invisible wires. He hit the canvas side of the wagon and left a wide smear of red as he slid lifelessly to the ground.

But Fargo had no time to get off a third shot as he saw an arrow hurtling straight at him. He had to duck, flatten himself across the Ovaro's neck as the shaft grazed his back. He looked up to see the Indian charging directly at him, his pony galloping full out. The Trailsman tried to bring the big Sharps up for another shot, realized he had time only to swing the stock of the rifle up to parry a vicious swing of a tomahawk. The blade of the short-handled ax hit the rifle with such force that Fargo felt himself fall sideways from his horse. He hit the ground on his back, shot a quick glance across at the wagon, and saw the fourth Indian pulling the girl onto his pony. "Damn," he spit out as he felt the hoofbeats thundering toward him. He rolled and saw the tomahawk slide along the side of his temple as the Indian delivered a swooping blow. He rolled, ended up on his back to see that the brave had already spun his pony around.

Fargo managed to pull the Colt from its holster as the red man charged at him again. On his back, he fired from the hip as the charging horse bore down on him. He saw the rider suddenly quiver and a red hole explode in the center of his chest. The man toppled forward with a guttural cry, landed facedown on the ground, and lay still. Fargo pushed backward, flung a glance at the wagon, and saw the fourth brave disappear into the trees on his pony, his arms wrapped around the young woman.

Fargo swung to his feet and ran to the Ovaro. A long upward dive put him in the saddle and the powerful horse was in full gallop in seconds.

He didn't slow as he raced into the trees, confident of the Ovaro's ability to maneuver and keep his speed. He gained ground quickly and saw the flaxen hair through the trees, a bouncing yellow beacon. He could hear the heavy breathing of the Indian pony as it slowed, its short-legged, barrel-chested body too chunky to skirt the dense trees. Fargo glimpsed the Indian make a sharp swerve to the right and disappear into a heavy cluster of box elder. He followed, the Ovaro deftly slipping between two tree trunks.

Fargo plunged into the box elder and suddenly yanked the horse to a halt. He could hear the Indian pony, but the animal was drawing in deep breaths of air. The red man had stopped. Fargo cursed and dived from the saddle as two arrows slammed into the tree trunk barely inches away from him.

He hit the ground on his side, winced at the impact, but rolled and came up with the Colt in his hand, fired two shots into the trees, and dropped to one knee. He caught the movement of brush to his right and the Colt was aimed at the spot as the Indian emerged, the young woman held in front of him, a hunting knife against her throat. He halted and pressed the edge of the knife blade to her skin until a trickle of red appeared. He barked a command and Fargo didn't need to understand the language to get the message. He hesitated a moment and saw the terror in the girl's eyes. With a silent curse, the Trailsman tossed the Colt onto the ground.

The Indian flung the young woman away instantly and charged forward, the hunting knife held out-stretched. Fargo's eyes stayed on the blade as he counted off seconds; he let the charging figure come a few steps closer, and as the point of the knife seemed about to plunge into his chest, he dropped almost to his knees. The Indian bowled into him and Fargo rose, slammed one shoulder into the man's abdomen, and the square, stocky form stag-gered back with a grunt of pain. Fargo swung a long, looping left that caught the man alongside his jaw and the Indian staggered backward again.

The Trailsman sprang forward to deliver a hard right, cursed at himself as he realized he'd been too hasty. The hunting knife was coming at him in an upward arc and he managed to twist his head to one side and felt the blade whistle past the tip of his jaw. He flung himself sideways and a slashing sweep of the knife just missed ripping into his shoulder. He hit the ground facedown, rolled, and came up on one knee to see his foe coming at him with quick, agile foot movements.

The Indian feinted and Fargo reacted, twisting away from another blow of the knife and letting himself seem to stumble back off-balance. With a roar of triumph, his opponent leapt forward, the hunting knife upraised. But the big man suddenly stopped stumbling backward. Instead, he dropped low as the knife slashed empty air over his head. He brought up a pile-driver uppercut that crashed into the red man's jaw. The Indian staggered back, tried to shake sudden cobwebs from his head. Fargo's left arm shot out, his hand closing around the Indian's wrist. He twisted and the hunting knife fell from the man's fingers.

Fargo flung the man aside and dived for the knife on the ground. He had just closed his fingers around the hilt when he felt the figure coming at him from behind. There was no time to turn or look around; he lashed out in a backhanded blow with the knife. He felt it connect and heard the gargled sound as the Indian fell half atop him. He sprang to his left and felt the man's body slide away and he whirled to see the Indian futilely pawing at his throat with one hand as his life's blood poured out. The man fell to both knees, still making strangled sounds, and finally pitched onto his face. He quivered for another moment and then lay still.

Fargo threw the knife into the underbrush and turned to see the young woman on one knee. She pushed to her feet as he reached her, breasts straining the neckline of the dress as she drew in deep gulps of air. The fear began to leave her eyes as he led her to the Ovaro and swung into the saddle behind her.

It wasn't until they returned to the wagon that she spoke. "Is it over?"

"I think so, but I'm not going to take any chances," Fargo said as he peered down at the still forms on the ground. He grunted. "Chippewa. I figured as much," he said. "They're not real bad, but they're not real friendly, either. Let's get out of here."

"I've something to say," she answered.

"Later," he said. "Take the reins." He watched as she stepped into the wagon with a graceful movement, and he motioned to an opening in the trees.

"I was going north," she said.

"Not now. Others might come looking for these. We take cover. Besides, you've less than an hour of daylight left," he said, and moved forward to lead the way into the woods.

He found openings barely wide enough for the big Owensboro and he watched with satisfaction as the fresh forest grass quickly sprang back to obliterate tracks. The forest grew thicker and the dusk quickly turned it into a place of shadowy shapes that made further travel dangerous. When the front corner of the wagon splintered against a tree, he called a halt. "This'll do. We're in far enough." he said. "No fire."

He dismounted, unsaddled the Ovaro, and leaned back against a tree trunk in the dimness. He felt the dampness of the night seep through the forest. An edge of wind reminded him that he had seen the last of the downy foxglove and oxeye daisies a few days ago. The bright red of the cardinal flower and the purple-fringed orchid, too. It would be up to the deep pink of the morning glory and the black-eyed Susan to bring color to the land now. He saw the shadowy form swing from the wagon and come toward him, the flaxen hair pale silver in the last of the dark dusk.

"You saved my life, Fargo. I can't ever repay that. But I owe you a very big apology and I can do something about that," she said.

"I'll settle for an explanation," Fargo answered. "I want to know what in hell you're doing out in this country all by yourself."

She settled against the tree trunk next to him and he smelled the faint muskiness of her, a mixture of powder and perspiration, somehow strangely attractive. "It wasn't supposed to be this way," she began.

2

"I'm supposed to be part of a seven-wagon train that left Colepoint five days ago," she said. "But I developed axle trouble. I learned it'd take three to four days to fix and I asked them to wait. But Wade Barnum refused."

"Who's Wade Barnum?"

"He's the scout for the train. He said they couldn't afford a four-day delay, the weather and schedule wouldn't allow it."

"I can see why he'd be concerned about weather, especially if you're going north. Winter can come real sudden," Fargo said.

"I offered to pay him extra for waiting, but he refused," she said.

"So you waited, got your axle fixed, and then took off to catch up to them."

"That's right," she said. "I was following their wagon tracks. I knew it was dangerous to go alone, but I thought I could catch up to them before anything happened. It seems I was wrong."

"You've a name," he remarked.

"Robin. Robin Carr," she said.

He smiled. It went with the blue of her eyes.

The night had descended, moonless and chilly, and the woods had become a totally black, stygian place. She was now a disembodied voice from beside him.

"What happens tomorrow?" he asked.

"I go on after them. I was making good time," Robin said.

"You were lucky today," Fargo commented.

"Thanks to you," she said. "Will you stay with me until I catch up to them? It shouldn't be more than a few days."

"We'll talk more in the morning," he said. "I'm going to find my gear and hit the bedroll."

"I sleep in the wagon. I've a mattress there," she said. He started to move from the tree when her hand reached out and found his arm. "Thank you again for today," she said, a softness in her voice that he'd not heard before. "I can't ever repay you, you know that," she added.

"Forget it. Besides, wheels have a way of coming around," he said, and her hand dropped from his arm. He heard her start to grope her way through the blackness and he did the same, found his gear, quickly undressed, and crawled into the bedroll. He listened to her inside the wagon until she fell silent. He drifted into sleep in the impenetrable blackness of the forest as a skulk of red foxes chattered in the distance.

He woke with the new day to find the sky still gray. He used his canteen to wash and had just finished when Robin stepped from the wagon. She sent a shower of yellow as she brushed her flaxen hair, and the drab brown dress couldn't hide the gracefulness of her slender figure as she swung to the ground.

" 'Morning," she said, and he smiled. She was trying to be polite but the question hung in her eyes.

"Ask it," he grunted. The sheepishness in her smile was very little-girl-like and very attractive. There was a lot of uncertainty under all that determination, he suspected.

"All right, will you stay with me until I catch up to the others?" she asked.

"I guess I can take the time for that," he said.
"I'll pay you."

"No," he said, dismissing the suggestion.

"What were you doing out here, Fargo?"

"On my way to a meeting in Lakeside," he said.

"That's up in the north country, isn't it?" she asked, and he caught the note of excitement that came into her voice.

"Not real north. More east," he said as he swung the saddle onto the Ovaro. "Get your things together and let's move," he said. When she was ready, he led the way out of the forest, taking a long circle that finally brought them onto the open land almost a half-mile farther on. He dismounted and ran his fingers over the edges of the wagon ruts in the ground. "You did make good time. These aren't much more than a day or so old," he said.

Robin Carr frowned at him. "You know about tracking?" she asked.

"A little." He grinned. "Some call me the Trailsman."

Her eyes grew rounder as a tiny gasp escaped her lips. "Oh, my. I am lucky," she murmured. "I want to hire you."

"I told you, there's no need for that," he said.

"Not for now. For later."

"Whoa, there. Slow down," he said. He climbed back on the pinto and swung alongside the wagon as they followed the tracks. "Tell me about Robin Carr. There are a lot of things that don't add up."

"Such as?"

"If you didn't have your axle troubles, you'd be with the rest of the wagons. But it looks to me as though you'd still be alone, 'less you've kin in the other wagons," Fargo said.

"No kin," Robin said. "And, yes, I *am* alone. I joined the wagon train at Colepoint because it was going north a little ways. But it's turning west near

Lake Itaca to go into the Dakotas. I'm leaving it there to go on north."

"Alone?" He frowned.

"I planned to hire a guide or a scout to take me. Maybe that's been solved now." She smiled.

"Take you where?"

"Into the north country, beyond Upper Red Lake."

"What in hell would you be going there for, all on your own?"

"To study the effects of winter on wildlife, especially the larger animals. I'm a naturalist. I studied with one of the great naturalists of all time, Professor Robert Welby. Before he died, he gave me the deed to a cabin he has up in the north country—a fine, sturdy place, he said. He knew I'd use it to carry on his work." She halted and tossed him a proud glance full of shining excitement. A furrow touched her brow as she saw him staring at her. "What's the matter?" she questioned.

"Nothing, except that the list of damn fools has grown bigger and better," he said, and saw the robin's-egg-blue eyes flare.

"I've made plans and considered everything," she said.

"You've made plans," he echoed, and let sarcasm coat each word. "Hell, honey, you don't have the foggiest notion of what you're getting into." He paused and glanced at the fescue grass that spread out beneath them. "Fact is, old man winter's already stretching his hands out. You want to do this, you'd have to start in the spring, and even then you couldn't do it. You'd need to spend all summer just cutting firewood."

"I expect I'll have enough time to lay in a good supply," she said.

"How are you going to get food to stay alive?"

"My wagon's crammed full of canned food and

dried meat, enough to last most of the winter. I'll shoot small game to fill in the rest," she returned.

"What if there is no small game?"

"There's always small game, snowshoe hare, that kind of thing."

"Like hell there is. And even if there is, you mightn't be able to bring it down. You can get so snowed in you can't dig out for weeks," Fargo said. "You ever see a north-country winter, honey?" Her shrug was an admission. "A grizzled old woodsman with thirty years' experience might make it through. Might. That leaves you coming up awfully short."

"I've confidence in myself. The people who make things happen are those with confidence in themselves, those who refuse to be frightened away. Lewis and Clark, Daniel Boone, James Bridger, Zeb Pike, James Audubon," she said. "Everyone told them they were crazy, too."

"There's one difference," Fargo said, and she waited, her lips tight. "They knew what they were doing. They had a lot of experience before they set out. Dammit, girl, you want to learn to ride you don't start with a wild stallion."

"I guess you won't be helping me go north," Robin said.

"I knew a man who wanted to kill himself once. I didn't help him either," Fargo said.

She tossed a glare of reproof at him. "You can go on now. You don't have to stay with me. I'll catch up to the others on my own."

"I said I'd stay for that," Fargo grunted. "Don't get uppity. You can't afford it."

Her glare softened. "I'm sorry," she said. "This is something I've wanted to do for so long, and I'm not going to turn away from it." She lapsed into silence as they rode.

He halted where a stand of wild apples would provide breakfast. The sky remained a chill gray as they went on and he found where the wagon train had camped for the night. The tracks were encouragingly fresh and they continued along the flat land as it rose to a long, uphill incline. The mountain ash still bordered both sides of the land with box elder growing heavier along the way.

Fargo cast a glance skyward as they started to climb the long rise of land. "It's fixing to rain hard," he muttered.

"Will we catch them before it does?" Robin asked.

"Not likely," he said as the slow rise grew steeper. They began to near the crest when Fargo motioned to halt as he saw the big black-winged shapes rise into the sky from the other side of the crest and slowly wheel in wide circles. He felt the instant chill cut into him. He had seen their ominous majesty too often. "Buzzards," he bit out.

"I know," Robin said as he watched the circling vultures. "Anything dead will attract them, an antelope, a horse."

He nodded. Her words were true enough, yet the chill inside him stayed, made of substance and shadow, premonitions and perceptions. Too many buzzards for a lone antelope. The location and time too disturbing. The fallibility of coincidence stabbed at him.

"Stay here. I'll go have a look," he said.

"No," he heard her say firmly, and he glanced at the young woman. "I'm not here to turn away from anything," Robin said.

He nodded and moved forward. She summoned her own strengths, he admitted. She'd sure as hell need them for what she was planning to do.

Fargo was riding beside the wagon as they crested the top of the rise, and he swore softly as his eyes peered down to the bottom of the other side of the incline. The six wagons were in a row, silent as a shroud, and he saw the forms hanging limply from the sides. He shot a glance at Robin and saw the tightness in her face as she stared at the scene. But she sent the wagon after him as he rode down the slope.

He slid from the horse when he reached the line of six wagons, mostly Conestogas, the canvas ripped away from all of them. He paused beside two arrows embedded in the tailgate of the last wagon, his gaze taking in the markings on each and the way in which the arrowheads were wrapped to the shafts.

"Assiniboin," he grunted. "Another breed of cat." He felt Robin's eyes on him as he slowly walked along the wagons and began to see where other men only looked, taking in the details that let him build sentences where others saw only words. He paused and saw Robin had left the wagon and was coming toward him.

"They were ambushed. They didn't have a chance. Look here, the wagons are all still in a straight line. They didn't have time to make a run for it or to turn their wagons to defend themselves," he said. He went on, peering into each wagon.

She followed, staying a half-dozen yards away. He felt the grimness clutching at him as he passed the buzzard-pocked silent bodies of men, women, and children. His eyes surveyed the contents of each wagon, not for what was there but what was no longer there. "They took blankets, shoes, some clothes, coats mostly, and rifles. There's not a rifle left in any of the wagons. That all pretty much figures."

Robin's hand went to her mouth as her voice broke. "And everyone dead. Everyone killed," she murmured. "Those savages!"

Fargo's gaze dropped to the ground. "Not everyone," he said. "Somebody got away." Robin's eyes widened and he pointed to the line of hoofprints that led away from the wagons and into the trees. Robin came to stand next to him. "Somebody got away," he repeated. "You up to telling me who?"

She stared at him for a long moment, drew a deep breath, and nodded. He held her arm as he walked from wagon to wagon with her and felt her fight the trembling inside her. She turned to him when they reached the last wagon. "Wade Barnum," she breathed. "He's the only one not here."

"That's the guide?" Fargo asked, and she nodded.

"It makes sense. He'd have been on horseback and able to run," Robin said.

Fargo's lips pursed as he dropped to one knee beside the hoofprints. "He didn't run," he said, and drew a frown from Robin.

"What do you mean?"

"A horse digs deep prints when he runs. This horse walked away from the wagons," Fargo said.

"How can that be? When did it walk away?" Robin stared.

"Can't say that. Maybe only minutes before the attack. I'd guess he went off to scout inside the trees. He probably picked up something, maybe a sound. He could have if he's any kind of a guide," Fargo said.

"And that's when the attack came."

"More than likely. I'd guess he saw it from inside the trees and knew there wasn't a thing he could do but save his hide," Fargo said, and pushed to his feet.

"Thank God somebody got away," Robin breathed.

"He wasn't the only lucky one," Fargo said. "You want to say a little prayer to a broken axle?"

The reality of his words drained the color from her face. "Yes. Oh, God, yes," she whispered, and stared into space for a long moment. She finally shook away the shattering realization and stared at the hoofprints of the lone horse. "Could we follow? Maybe catch up to him and find out exactly what happened?" she asked.

Fargo felt a sharp gust of wind and a handful of raindrops and sent a glance skyward. The grayness had turned deeper. "No time. I've got to find us a place to sit out this storm. But I want to unhitch the horses from these wagons first. They'll fend for themselves once they're free."

Robin nodded and helped unhitch the horses, which at first scattered, then gathered themselves into a herd and trotted away. She climbed back onto her wagon as Fargo motioned forward and rode on ahead of her.

He'd gone perhaps a thousand yards when he spied a break in the mountain ash and a steep slope. He waited for Robin to catch up before he rode up the slope as another gust of wind brought a shower of rain. He peered up to where the slope rose to a line of rocky ridges, and he spurred the pinto forward. He saw the long overhang of rock to the far right of the second ridge. It was long enough, and when he rode up to it, he saw that it was also deep enough. He rode to the back wall of rock at the deepest part of the overhang and dismounted.

Robin and the big Owensboro were still laboring up the sharp slope and he had firewood gathered and set in a dry place when she arrived.

She drove to the rear of the overhang beside the Ovaro and unhitched the team as he started a fire. It was growing dark quickly and the rain was coming down hard now, driven by a cold wind. Robin dropped to her knees beside the fire with a shiver and let the warmth reach out to her. The firelight danced in the yellowness of her hair.

Fargo took some dried-beef strips from his saddlebag, warmed them over the fire, and she ate hungrily beside him. The rock overhang kept the rain from reaching them even in the heaviest gusts of wind, and Robin stretched out beside the fire when they'd eaten. The soft glow of the fire gave her classic features a heightened beauty.

She glanced up to catch his eyes on her. "What are you thinking?"

"That you're damn attractive," he said bluntly.

"And damn stupid."

"Bull's-eye," he grunted.

She offered a wry smile. "What happens tomorrow, when the storm ends?"

"There'll be no following hoofprints after this rain," he said. "I'll find the nearest town for you."

She leaned toward him, her eyes round with sincerity. "Something good has to come out of what happened. Maybe it'll be my going on. I was spared. Maybe that was a sign to me to go on."

"Maybe it was a warning," he said.

"I saw the way you read signs back there. You're special. You could find the cabin for me. I've a kind of map, but it's pretty vague."

"I told you, I'm going to Lakeside for a meeting. It's been put off for years. I'm not putting it off again," he told her. "And I spoke my piece about that crazy plan of yours."

"So you did," she snapped, and fell silent. He let the fire burn low enough to cast a warm glow before he took down his sleeping gear.

"Time to get some shut-eye," he said, and Robin didn't stir. He shrugged and began to undress and saw her eyes move across the symmetry of his smoothly muscled torso. He was starting to undo his gun belt when she rose and went into the wagon. He was in his bedroll when she came from the Owensboro with her blanket and set it beside the fire.

"It's cold in there," she said. She wore a light-

29

blue nightdress, long and buttoned up high at the neck. It clung to her and outlined her slenderness. She lay down and pulled the blanket around her. "Fargo," she called softly, and he pushed up on one elbow. "I'm sorry to get so angry. You've been very wonderful. I just wish I could make you see things as I do."

"I just wish I could make you know what I know," he said, not urgently. "Now get some sleep."

"Good night," she murmured, and turned on her side.

He lay awake a little longer and wondered about fools and heroes. Maybe there wasn't much difference between them, only whether they failed or succeeded. He finally slept to the steady sound of the rain.

He rose twice during the night to add more wood to the fire. Robin slept restlessly and he heard her toss and turn, and the second time he tended the fire he saw that the blanket had fallen from around her shoulders. The high buttons of the nightdress had come open also, to let him glimpse the curve of one seemingly full white mound. He pulled the blanket back up around her shoulders and she stirred and made tiny sounds.

He returned to his bedroll and slept till the morning. He rose and watched the storm begin to wind down. He was washed and dressed when Robin woke, looking deliciously soft as she rubbed sleep from her eyes.

She gathered the blanket around herself and shuffled to the wagon. When she emerged, the brown dress had been replaced by a leather skirt and a tan shirt that pulled tight across the curves of full breasts. The skirt revealed a lean figure with a tight, trim rear and a lovely turn of calf.

The rain ended and the temperature grew crisp,

filled with the spirit of fall. The sun came out, but Robin's flaxen hair was its own sunburst.

Fargo helped her hitch the brace and then saddled the Ovaro. She was waiting atop the driver's seat of the Owensboro when he finished. "We'll go north a way and then east," he said.

"You might just as well leave me out here as in some dust-hole town where I'll never find a guide," she said, paused, and shot him a sidelong glance. "Or is that your plan, to leave me someplace where I'll never find a guide to take me into the north country?"

"Hadn't thought of that, but it's not a bad idea."

"Well, you can forget it, because I'll just go on alone."

"You'd be dumb enough," he agreed, and her eyes shot blue sparks at him.

"How can you be so very wonderful and so rotten?" she threw back.

"Practice," he said, snapping the reins. The Ovaro went into a trot that quickly left the wagon behind.

Some of what he'd said had struck home. It was behind her temper. She knew she tackled a damn big task. That was a good sign. But she held the dream too tightly just to let go. And, for good or bad, she had confidence in herself. He wouldn't push any harder than he had. She was the kind who needed time to think, reflect, and wrestle with herself. But he didn't have much hope she'd back away. His eyes swept the rolling land and he wished he knew the territory better.

He'd ridden the land before but not as far north. Minnesota, the Indians had named it, the place where the sky is in the land. Well-named, he reckoned as he caught the sky-blue sparkle of the sun on distant lakes on all sides of the land. It was a rich land, good soil, lakes filled with northern pike, white bass, and rainbow trout; a land teeming with game, beaver, badger, moose, and white-tailed deer; the gray wolf and the grizzly and sometimes the Alaskan Kodiak bear wandered down. But it was like a deceiving woman, offering riches with tempting ease only to extract a terrible price from those who were beguiled.

The Indian spent from spring to fall preparing for the fierce north winters. Even the hardiest of trappers retreated into town. They knew not to succumb to the blandishments of the land. They knew how quickly it could change from giving to killing.

Fargo saw Robin had slipped a shawl over her shoulders when she caught up to him and let a knowing smile touch his lips. "The wind's turned chilly," she sniffed.

"A message," Fargo said.

"Of what?"

"Winter's coming early."

"You'd say that, anyway," she returned. "Anything to make me think again about going on."

"I wish that's what I was doing," he said tightly, and drew to a halt beside a cluster of wild-cherry bushes.

Robin took out two johnnycakes and shared one with him as they munched both cake and cherries.

When they went on, he set a faster pace, but by midafternoon he'd seen only wandering tracks, some shod, more unshod, and nothing that pointed to any traffic toward a town. And they were not making good time. He changed his searching, and before a half-hour had passed, he found a secluded arbor of yellow poplar and led the way inside it.

"I need to ride alone, climb some high hills, make some time, and I can't do it with one eye on you and the wagon," he told Robin. "You just relax and rest here. We'll probably make camp here. You'll be safe. Stay in this arbor until I get back."

"When will that be?"

"I'll be back in an hour or two," he said, and she nodded, plainly grateful for the rest.

She was climbing from the wagon as he rode from the arbor and climbed the nearest hill. He searched the land from the top, looking for riders, a cabin, a camp fire. He found nothing but the slow-trudging motion of a moose and the chatter of chickadees. He turned east, rode up another hill, and found nothing to help him. In the far distance, where the land grew flat, he glimpsed the glistening thread of a river. It'd take another day's ride to reach it, but he marked it in his mind. He'd ride for it tomorrow if he found nothing better before.

He continued to ride and scan the ground close by and in the distance until he turned back while there was still daylight left. He guessed he'd been riding for almost two hours when he returned to the arbor and pushed through the trees to rein to a halt, his lips drawing back. The wagon wasn't there.

"Goddamn that girl," Fargo swore as he followed the tracks of the wagon where it had rolled from the arbor. She had driven down a small slope to the right; he followed, saw where she had swung into a sharp turn at the bottom of the slope. Some twenty yards on, he saw where she had halted and he also saw the hoofprints of three horses.

She had driven on, and the three horses had stayed with her. Fargo swore under his breath as he followed. The land stayed flat but suddenly turned into a fairly heavy growth of velvety-twigged red ash. The Trailsman saw where the wagon and the three horsemen moved in and out of the trees, threading their way forward. Then he suddenly glimpsed the big Owensboro halted some hundred yards ahead.

He slowed and melted beneath the branches of the nearest ash. He heard Robin before he saw her, a sharp cry, and then he spotted her a few yards to the right of the wagon. The three riders were with her, but all on foot now, two holding her arms while the third rubbed his hands across her breasts.

Fargo's eyes grew cold as an ice floe as he took in the three men. The one fondling the girl was the tallest, with dull, sandy hair and a sandy, straggly mustache. The other two were oafish-faced drifters, both with leering grins of anticipation.

The sandy-haired one began to unbutton Robin's shirt. She twisted, and though firmly held by the other two, she brought her knee up in a quick, sharp thrust. The mustached one cursed in pain even though he managed to avoid taking the blow full in the groin. He stepped back and mashed a hand across Robin's face.

"Goddamn bitch," he snarled, and snapped at the other two. "Throw her down and hold on to her, goddammit," he ordered.

They went down and pulled Robin with them. One held both her arms while the other pinned one of her legs with his.

"That's better," the sandy-haired one said, and dropped to his knees in front of Robin. He reached out and started to open her shirt further as Robin tried to twist free but with no success.

Fargo slid soundlessly from the saddle, the big Colt .44 in his hand.

"Regular little hellcat, isn't she?" the mustached one said as Fargo crept closer. He raised the Colt and his lips formed a grimace as he took in the scene again.

He could bring down the sandy-haired one with ease. But the other two were all over Robin. They'd instantly use her as a shield. Even if he got one, the other would have her, and he wanted to find a way to avoid that. He swore silently as he didn't see any way to prevent it. He couldn't take the two holding Robin first, not without risking Robin taking a bullet. He needed something to make them move away from her, something to take them all by surprise.

Suddenly a tight smile edged his lips. He turned to the Ovaro, raised his left hand, and brought it down on the horse's rump in a sharp slap. The pinto bolted at once, bursting forward into the open almost atop the three men and their captive. Fargo saw the two holding Robin push up from her in surprise while the sandy-haired one spun as he yanked at his gun.

Fargo fired three shots, which erupted with such speed that the sounds melted into one.

The sandy-haired man did a strange little dance as he spun and clutched at his abdomen, the gun falling from his hand. The one at Robin's right simply toppled back soundlessly as his forehead spurted red. The last man rolled away from Robin, tried to push to his feet, and managed only two steps before he pitched forward with a scream of pain as the third bullet smashed into his spine.

Robin was scooting backward, pushing to her feet, as Fargo stepped into the open. She saw him with eyes round as saucers and she half-fell, half-ran to bury her head into his chest. He held her for a moment, the flaxen hair half-covering his chin, before he pulled back.

"Get the wagon," he said coldly, and she nodded and hurried to the rig.

He climbed onto the pinto and led the way back to the little arbor in the last of the dusk. She wheeled the wagon against one side and he unsaddled the pinto before he faced her. "Now, tell me, you don't hear well or you can't follow orders?" he asked scathingly.

Her lips tightened. "I saw them below through

the trees. I thought perhaps they could give us directions."

"I told you to stay put."

'We were looking for help, remember?" she said defensively. "I thought I was doing the right thing."

"I know what you thought. That's the only reason I'm still here with you."

"I'm sorry," she said. "I made a mistake."

"You did," he grunted. "And when you're all by yourself in the middle of winter, any mistake will be your last one."

She looked away, but he saw his words mirrored in the tightness of her face. Finally she brought her eyes back to him. "If you'd seen them, you'd have gone out to ask directions," she said with a defensive stubbornness he had to admire.

"First, my going out asking wouldn't be the same as you," Fargo said, and her small shrug was agreement. "Then, I'd have looked them over before I rode out," he added.

"You'd have been able to tell about them by that?" Robin asked, wide-eyed again.

"Some things. Sometimes you can tell something about a man just by the way he sits his horse. Tracks and trails aren't all on the ground. A man carries his life in his face, his eyes, the way he stands and walks. So does a woman. I'd have seen those three as drifters. It was in their way as well as their cracked saddle leather and run-down boots," Fargo said.

"What do I carry in my face, in the way I stand?" Robin asked, a sly smile touching her lips.

"You haven't been around long enough to carry much," he answered. "Now let's eat. I'm hungry."

He made a small fire as the night came, a crispness in it again, and a new moon sent just enough light to take the total blackness from the little arbor. They combined a can of beans and some beef jerky to make a satisfying meal, and he took his bedroll down as the fire burned low. He started to shed his shirt when Robin came to him.

"Thank you," she murmured. "For coming after me. It seems all I do is say thank you to you."

"Paying some heed to good advice might put a stop to that," he remarked.

Her sheepish shrug was an admission, and he saw her eyes searching his face. "You deserve more than words. I'm sorry I'm just not that kind of person," she said.

"You hear me complain any?"

"No, but I'm sure you're just being nice."

"Or patient," he remarked blandly.

Tiny dots of color burst into her cheeks and she turned away and hurried to the wagon.

He was undressed and in his bedroll when she returned with her blanket, the blue nightdress cloaking her again, but this time she had left the top buttons open. He smiled inwardly. Signs? he wondered. If so, they were the kind she was unaware of herself, he was certain.

She settled herself and the fire burned out.

When morning came, she was sleeping half out of the blanket in a shaft of sunlight. Again, he enjoyed the curve of one white breast that edged over the neckline of the nightdress. Asleep, she looked very girllike, but the inner strength was there in the strong cheekbones and the classic lines of her face.

It would be a tragedy to leave her to the winds and wolves of the north winter. He'd not let that happen if he could stop it. His greatest ally was her own intelligence, he realized; his greatest enemy her dreams and determination. He rose and dressed, not at all certain which would win.

3

The horses were lively in the crisp morning air and Fargo set a strong pace for the distant river he had spotted the day before. Riding some hundred yards ahead of the wagon, he watched the land as it rolled in gentle hills with thick growths of shagbark hickory, box elder, and red ash. He was passing a line of the red ash when he caught the movement in the high brush atop a hillock to his right. He slowed, peered, and the brush moved again, something half-rising from it to sink down immediately. Too big for small game, he thought. Perhaps it might be a coyote. But he decided to take no chances on being attacked from behind. He turned the pinto toward the hillock and moved slowly, one hand resting atop the revolver on his hip.

The brush moved again, directly in front of him, and he had the Colt in his hand as he nosed the horse into the brush. He reined up suddenly to find himself staring down at a child, a little girl of not more than six years of age, he guessed. She wore sandals and a torn brown dress, and she stared up at him with strange eyes that seemed to be both blank and fearful. He swung from the pinto as the child rose and continued to stare at him. Her round-cheeked face was smudged, her brown hair uncombed, and her legs were streaked with tiny lines of dried blood from thorn and briar cuts. He took a step toward her. She stiffened and he thought she might bolt away.

"It's all right," he said softly. "It's all right." The child continued to stare at him with the strange eyes, but the fright had gone from her body, he saw. He reached out and put a hand on her tiny shoulder. "What are you doing way out here?" he asked. She didn't answer. "What's your name?" he tried, and again he received no answer. Carefully, he closed both hands around her waist. "Why don't we take a ride?" he said, and lifted her up.

She didn't resist. She didn't say anything. She didn't utter any kind of sound.

He turned, sat her in the saddle, and swung up behind her. She sat quietly as he slowly moved the pinto from the hillock and reached the flat land below as Robin and the wagon came along. Robin's eyes widened as she pulled the horses to a stop. "Found her up there in the brush," Fargo said. "From the look of her, I'd say she's lost and been that way for at least a week, maybe more."

Robin smiled at the child. "Hello," she said. "What's your name?" The little girl made no answer and stared back with her strange expression. "My name's Robin," Robin tried, and received not a sign of any response. She glanced at Fargo. "She's in some kind of shock," Robin said. "Something must've happened to whoever was with her."

"Seen a child like this before," Fargo said. "Heard of a few others. Some never talked again. Others finally did." He didn't tell Robin what had made them that way.

"We'll have to take her with us," Robin said. "Till we find a town."

Fargo took the little girl by the waist again with both hands and swung her onto the seat of the wagon beside Robin. She offered no resistance and seemed perfectly willing to go along with whatever they wanted. But there was no sound from her and her eyes continued to stare with their strangely blank expression.

She sat unmoving as Robin took up the reins and sent the wagon forward. "How'd she stay alive out here alone for a week? Or more?" Robin asked.

"She probably stayed in the brush most of the time. There's plenty of fruit, nuts, and water here. And she was lucky," Fargo said.

"Poor little thing," Robin murmured. She tried communicating with the child again with no result.

Fargo rode alongside as the land turned into a long, slow curve with hickory lining both sides. They had almost reached the end of the curve when Fargo's nostrils drew in the odor, cloying yet acrid, a stomach-turning pungency to it he had smelled all too often. He turned to Robin in time to see the little girl leap up and vault from the seat into the back of the wagon.

"Stay here," Fargo snapped.

"What is it?" Robin frowned. "What's that awful odor?"

"Stay," Fargo repeated, and started to ride on.

"No," Robin called. "I told you, I'm not turning away from anything."

He rode on without answering. Let her follow, he muttered silently. She wanted to toughen up. This would sure as hell do it. He reached the end of the curve to see the line of wagons near a cluster of ash. No buzzards now. They had long gone, finished with their gouging and picking. Only the terrible, sickening odor of human flesh decomposing under the hot sun.

He held his breath as he reached the wagons, five of them, and he halted as he heard Robin come to the end of the curve. He looked back, saw her clutching the reins as she averted her gaze. She leaned half over one side of the wagon and retched, and he remembered the first time he'd come on such a sight and smell.

She straightened up, peered across at him, and he motioned for her to stay away and go on. He waited as she made a wide circle along the edge of the trees, putting the brace into a trot until she halted, almost out of sight.

Fargo moved to the wagons, swept each one with a slow gaze as he rode past. He took in every detail inside the wagons as he scanned the ground on both sides also. No horses left. They'd broken loose of their harnesses, he noticed by the torn strips of leather and splintered shaft ends.

The partly skeletal remains of what had once been human beings littered the wagons and the ground. In some instances, only clothing let him know which had been a man, which had been a woman, which a child. He halted at the lead wagon and his eyes fell upon a small black leather-covered book alongside what had been a young girl. A dress and bright hair ribbon told him that much. The small, leather-bound black book bore the gold-stamped word DIARY, and he reached out and took it from the wagon. He paused a minute more to survey the scene again with his eyes narrowed, and finally he turned away and rode to where Robin had halted and sat ghostly white on the big Owensboro. The wind blew east and they were beyond the sickening odor as Robin's eyes found him, pain and questions inside their roundness.

"The child," he said.

"Inside," Robin answered.

"Move on," he ordered grimly, and she snapped the reins over the horses. He rode beside her in silence until they had gone another quarter-mile on and over a shallow rise and down the other side. "Now you know why the child doesn't talk," he said as he drew to a halt.

"She was part of the wagon train. My God," Robin murmured.

"This attack was at least three to four weeks ago," Fargo said. "Assiniboin. Probably the same ones who hit your wagons. They took rifles, coats, the same things. The wagons were ambushed, hit so hard and so fast they didn't have a chance to run or make a circle to defend themselves."

"Same as with my wagon train," Robin said.

"That's right," Fargo grunted.

"But only the child got away this time," Robin said.

"Didn't find any prints to say otherwise. But the ground around the wagons was too chewed up to find any," Fargo said.

Robin nodded to the book in his hand. "What's that?"

"Diary. Took it from the first wagon," he answered, and opened the book. "My diary . . . Sally Brightson," he read aloud. "August tenth. We left Tar Hills today and followed Pebble River till late afternoon, when we turned east. Everybody was excited and stayed up late after we camped for the night." Fargo paused and turned to the next page. "August eleventh. This is fun. Coming from Arkansas, I've never seen land or animals like this. It's probably the greatest adventure I'll ever have." Fargo stopped and flipped through the next few pages. "The last entry is August fourteenth. That means they were only five days out of Tar Hills when they were massacred," he said.

"Which means Tar Hills can't be that far away," Robin said, excitement coming into her voice. "We have to get the little girl there. Maybe there'll be a doctor or relatives there. Maybe just friends of her folks'."

Fargo snapped the diary shut. It made a thudding sound, not unlike the closing of a casket. Robin peeked inside the wagon. "She all right?" Fargo asked.

"Curled up in a corner, staring at nothing," Robin said.

"Let's roll," Fargo growled. He set a fast pace for the rest of the day, cutting across the ground at an angle to reach the distant river. By late afternoon he found a shallow waterway filled with small rocks. "Pebble River," he grunted, and followed its swerving course south.

When night came, he camped along the shoreline and watched as the child let Robin wash her without uttering a sound. Cleaned and dried, she accepted some food and then disappeared inside the big Owensboro.

"I feel sick every time I look at her," Robin said. "My God, what a savage land."

"What's right to some is savage to others. Every settler is a threat, an intruder, an enemy out to take the land. That's what the Indian sees and that's what he answers in his own ways," Fargo said, and took down his bedroll.

The night turned colder and the flat land stretched out beyond the stony river, the sky a dark-blue blanket with twinkling silver sequins.

Robin changed inside the wagon and returned with her blanket to lay almost at his side. "I know what you're thinking," she said, and he rose on one elbow to look over at her.

"Tell me," he said.

"You're thinking this is all using up valuable time for me and I don't have any to use up. And you're happy about that," she said, sitting up.

"Every little bit helps," he admitted.

"Well, I'll make up the time. Maybe I can find a trail guide in Tar Hills."

"I've news for you, Robin. Experienced trail guides are hard to come by," he said, enjoying the way the long curve of one breast pressed up from the edge of the top of the nightdress as she turned to him.

"Maybe I'll get lucky and find one," she snapped.

"Maybe you'll get lucky and not find one."

"Good night," she hissed, and pulled the blanket around herself.

Fargo went to sleep quickly, and when morning came, the child ate two apples and sat on the seat next to Robin. But she remained utterly silent as Fargo followed the river south.

It was noon when the buildings of the town rose up, some two hundred yards east of the river. Four small hills formed a backdrop to the town, which spread out and became larger than it first seemed.

They passed a row of neatly tended houses and swung onto a wide main street with plenty of traffic, but Fargo noted that there was a larger-than-usual number of surreys and buckboards mixed in with work wagons. The town held a good collection of stores, from feed shops to barber shops. When he saw a knot of well-dressed figures in front of a building with the sign TOWN MEETING HALL, he reined to a halt. Robin stopped beside him as he called out, "Excuse me, is there a doc in town?" he asked.

One of the men, well-dressed in an afternoon coat of gray with a ruffled shirt, stepped forward. "Yes, Doc Darby, other end of town," he said, and paused to stare at the child. "That's little Annie Johnson, Ben and Mary's girl," he said.

Fargo exchanged quick glances with Robin. "They were part of the wagon train that left here about a month back?" he asked the man.

"Yes," the man said, and the others moved closer. "Why? What's happened?"

"She's the only one left," Fargo said quietly. "And she's been struck mute." He watched the shock travel through the faces of the small knot of people.

"Oh, God. Oh, my God," a woman cried out.

"Get Grandpa Johnson," the man said, and one of the other men hurried away. "I'm Tim Bryan of the town council," the man said to Fargo. "You sure about what you're saying, mister?"

"Name's Fargo and I'm sure, too damn sure," the big man spit out bitterly.

Bryan stepped to the wagon and spoke to the child. "Annie, it's Mr. Bryan. You're safe now," he said, but the child only stared at him. He turned back to Fargo. "Everyone?" he asked, shock still in his face.

"Everyone." Fargo nodded. "It was fast. No torturing," he added, weak words for comfort but they were all he could offer. Bad news travels fast, and when the man who'd gone off returned, he had another cluster of people with him. One, a bald old man with kindness in a weathered face, rushed to the child.

"Annie, it's me, Grandpa," he said. He reached up and lifted her from the wagon. She made no sign of protest or of greeting, her small face set into its soundless stare as if in stone. "Good God, I'll get her right over to the doc," the old man said, and hurried off with the child.

The others gathered around Fargo and Robin with pain-filled questions. He answered without softening. They deserved the truth, and the dead deserved no less.

"We're indebted to you both for saving the child and bringing her back," Tim Bryan said.

"Such a terrible tragedy," a woman intoned. "They were all so happy, all so full of hope for a new life."

"And that young trail guide, so full of confidence, making sure they left right on time," another woman said. "Such a handsome young man, so tall, with all that reddish hair and blue eyes."

Fargo heard Robin cut in. "Reddish hair, very tall, and good-looking?" she echoed, and he saw the crease come into her brow.

"Yes, Wayne Dumont," the woman said.

"You mean Wade Barnum," Robin said.

"No, Wayne Dumont. He always wore a leather vest with the letter W stitched into it," the woman said.

"That's Wade Barnum," Robin insisted, and Fargo saw her eyes turn to him and he silenced the question in them.

"We'll be moving on," he said to the others. "Sorry for the news we brought." They offered a murmur of gratitude and he walked the pinto on down the wide street until he halted some fifty yards on in front of a white clapboard building that proclaimed itself the Tar Hills Inn.

Robin halted beside him and the frown had deepened on her brow. "Something's wrong. Something's very wrong, and I don't understand it. That was Wade Barnum she described," Robin said.

"You sure?"

"Yes, absolutely."

"Strange things happen. Coincidences."

"Two very tall, good-looking trail guides with reddish hair?" Robin sniffed.

"It's just possible."

"Both wearing a leather vest with the letter W stitched into it?" she scoffed.

"That does stretch it damn far," he admitted.

"Indeed, but then, it doesn't add up. These wagons were attacked almost a month before my train," Robin said.

"And if he were killed in this attack with the others, he couldn't have been the guide with your train," Fargo said, paused, and let his lips purse.

"Unless," he said, and let the single word hang in midair. Robin waited, her lips parted. "Unless the little girl wasn't the only survivor," Fargo finished.

"We assumed she was. I didn't go over each wagon with you," Robin said. "Maybe we assumed wrongly."

"There's only one way to be sure," Fargo said. "I'll go back and look for a leather vest with a W stitched into it."

"I'll go with you."

"No. I'll make it in half the time on my own," Fargo said. "Take a room at the inn. It'll give you a chance to find that guide. I'll come back and tell you what I found, promise."

Fargo turned, put the Ovaro into a trot, and rode away. He kept at a steady pace until he camped for the night under a wide butternut. He lay awake after eating and wondered what strange turn of events he had gotten himself into. Whatever it was, he'd let others follow it through, he muttered. He was expected in Lakeside and he'd not come this far to change plans. He drew sleep to himself and was in the saddle with the first light of the new day.

Taking shortcuts across low hills and holding a steady trot, he reached the grim scene by early afternoon, the sickeningly pungent odor still clinging in the air. He moved slowly along the line of wagons, peering into each. Clothing was the only means of identification left, with maybe some jewelry, and he scanned the small piles of fabric that lay listlessly over the remains of what had been men, women, and children. He let his glance linger at each, and when he reached the last wagon, he turned the Ovaro in a wide circle.

"No leather vest," he muttered aloud as he began to ride back along the shore of Pebble river. "No leather vest." The words danced inside him, their meaning still unclear.

But he refused to explore the dark thoughts that stabbed at him. There'd be time for that. He'd let those evolve of themselves and talk to Robin again before he opened up a cave of horror. He rode steadily into the night and reached Tar Hills a little past the midnight hour. He secured a good corner stall for the Ovaro at the public stable and paid to have him given a good currying, come morning. He took a room at the inn and enjoyed the comfort of a bed. When morning came, he went downstairs to find Robin waiting outside the inn.

"I went to the stable to check on my horses and saw your Ovaro," she said a little smugly, and he saw the waiting form in the robin's-egg-blue eyes.

"No leather vest," he said. "I'd say Wayne Dumont got away."

"And as Wade Barnum he came to Colepoint and took out another wagon train," Robin said.

"It seems that way," Fargo said.

"I suppose if a man makes a living as a trail guide, he wouldn't stop just because he escaped an Indian attack," Robin suggested.

"He'd say something about the attack on the last train if he were a proper trail guide. It'd be his duty," Fargo said.

"Maybe he figured we wouldn't go on, then. That'd be putting himself out of a job," Robin said.

"No, this doesn't hinge on that kind of logic. There's something very wrong about all of it. A man doesn't survive an Indian attack and keep quiet about it. It's too shattering an experience. I never knew anybody who didn't talk about his good luck, at least. But this man goes to another town and takes out another train, using a different name. And then he somehow manages to walk away from the second attack and disappears."

Robin's eyes were darkened. "What are you saying?"

"I'm thinking it was more than just luck that he was the only survivor of both attacks, not counting you or the little girl."

"You saying that he . . ." Robin began, and floundered for words, the horror of the thought suddenly overwhelming her.

"Deliberately led both those wagon trains into being massacred," Fargo said. "It'd also explain why they never had a chance to make a run for it or close a circle. Neither were the usual Indian attacks. They were ambushes, traps they rode into."

"My God, why? Why would a man do a thing like that? Why in God's name?"

Fargo uttered a grim sound. "Men have always more reasons for doing bad than good."

"We have to do something about him."

"I have to get to Lakeside."

Robin looked aghast. "And let a man like that go on?"

Fargo speared her with a jaundiced stare. "How do you figure to catch him? You going to go to every little town in the state and hope you get lucky?" he asked, and she glowered back. "And if you find him, you couldn't prove a damn thing."

"But you know what he's done. You spelled it out yourself," she protested.

"Suspecting isn't enough. Knowing inside doesn't mean shit. Proof is all that counts, and you've no proof of anything. There's no law against a man saving his neck by running from an attack. You can't prove he led those wagons into a death trap, no matter what you know inside you."

"There must be some way to stop him," Robin said, a note of despair in her voice now.

"Maybe he'll make a mistake. Or somebody else someplace else will come on to him. But I'm going to Lakeside. As for you, if you lose one more day, you'll never make the north country in time, I can damn well promise you that. So you've got a choice, honey. You can put aside your conscience or your dreams."

"It's not fair to put it that way. This man is some kind of monster," Robin said.

"Whoever said life was fair," Fargo answered. "Your call, honey."

He saw the emotions turn and twist and fight inside her. They were there in the strain in her face and her clenched hands. She stared into space, pain pulling on the classic lines of her face. Finally she turned to him. "I'm going on north. I hate myself for it, but I have to go on," she said, paused, and peered at him. "It's not just being selfish. You said it yourself. I'd have to go looking for every little town and hope to get lucky and then get proof."

"So I did." He nodded. "You get yourself a trail guide yet?"

"I went to Councilman Bryan. He has someone for me. I'm on my way to meet him now," she said.

"Good. Then you're all set. I'll be riding on," he said.

She blinked and stepped forward with a sudden, quick movement and he felt her lips on his, smooth softness, and then she pulled away. "Thank you, for everything," she murmured.

"Too bad there wasn't more time," he said, and she frowned. "I've still got some patience left." The tiny dots of color touched her cheekbones again.

"I wish I could hate you for not helping me," she murmured.

"Work on it," he said, and laughed. She turned away with a mixture of sadness and irritation in her eyes. He walked to the stable and retrieved the Ovaro, inspected the magnificent horse with a quick, practiced eye. They'd done a fair job of currying, as good as he could expect from a public stable, and he walked back to the inn to pay his bill, the horse following at his heels. They were serving breakfast at the inn, he found, and he had coffee and eggs and biscuits in a large ground-floor room that was obviously used as a dining room in the evenings.

He was aware of the small knot of uncomfortableness that lay inside him. Guilt was so damn hard to reason away, even with the best logic. Barnum or Dumont, or whatever his name was, was a special kind of killer, a cold-blooded, sick monster. Robin had been right on that. Fargo felt his mouth tighten. He couldn't go around chasing down every killer in the West, no matter how much they deserved catching. He'd done his share of that. Somebody else would have to do it on this one.

He finished the last of the biscuits and went outside just in time to see Robin passing. She halted as he came toward her.

"It's all set. I have a trail guide," she said a little smugly, and paused.

"If you're expecting congratulations, you'll have a long wait," he said.

"I wasn't expecting congratulations," she sniffed.

"No, but you'd have liked them."

"It's a nephew of Mr. Bryan's, Ted Maxwell. He's young and Mr. Bryan says he has a natural talent for tracking. He's honest, reliable, the kind of person I could feel safe with."

"Sounds like a lot of words to cover up no experience," Fargo commented.

"He has experience. He took a seven-wagon train only a few months ago," Robin said. "He's meeting me at the stable. Come along if you like."

Fargo shrugged and fell in step beside her. "Why not? I'm curious. It's one of my failings," he said.

They reached the stable and waited while Robin had the brace brought out and hitched to the

Owensboro. Fargo took the opportunity to peer behind the canvas top and saw the boxes of canned goods she had stored in the wagon. They left her barely enough room for the mattress and the dried meat hung in wax-paper strips from the wagon bows. He pulled his head out as he heard Robin talking to someone; he saw a young man, hardly more than a boy, short brown hair and a smooth-skinned face with round brown eyes. He had an open, trustful face, the kind of face that inspired everything but confidence.

"This is Ted Maxwell, Fargo," Robin introduced.

"Robin told me how you helped her. You're the one they call the Trailsman," Ted Maxwell said with awe in his voice.

"Some do," Fargo said. "I hear you took out a seven-wagon train a few months ago. Where'd you go?"

"South and then east across the St. Croix into Wisconsin," the young man said. He offered a half-apologetic shrug. "It's not hard country," he said, and Fargo nodded. He didn't push the admission. There was no need. The boy knew how little he knew and Fargo wondered if perhaps his uncle hadn't pushed him into this.

"Good luck," Fargo said, and watched Ted walk to where the dull brown mare and a packhorse waited. He turned and met Robin's eyes, defiant and questioning at once.

"Go on, say whatever you're thinking," she snapped.

"I'm thinking this is the deaf leading the blind," he said.

"Damn you, Fargo," she hissed, and he shrugged as she went, the wagon rolling almost over his foot. "We'll do just fine," she flung back, and he watched her go on with Ted Maxwell alongside.

Fargo's lips were a thin line as he drew a deep

sigh. Damn her stubborn hide, he muttered silently. She was the worst kind. She involved you without talking. No female wiles, no smooth-talking guile. That'd be easier to turn away from. Her kind reached with the power of the innocent. They made you remember when you were full of faith and hope. They drew you in out of your own yesterdays.

Damn her, he repeated, and rode slowly from town, took a path into the low rolling hills where he could see the wagon below through the black oak. He watched Ted Maxwell ride ahead and find small, low-lying passages the wagon could easily negotiate. He did well enough, Fargo conceded.

When the day ended and the wagon drew into a tree-lined place to camp, Fargo settled down in the hills above and slept quickly when night descended.

He was in the saddle and watching as Ted and Robin prepared to move on when morning came. The youth led the way to a plateau, fairly flat and only sparsely dotted with black oak. Ted rode on ahead of Robin.

Fargo wandered down to the plateau and hung back far enough, barely able to see the big Owensboro. Morning slid into the early afternoon when he saw Ted Maxwell appear, racing the mare hard back to the wagon. The Trailsman watched Ted gesture excitedly and Robin followed him as she turned the wagon sharply to the right. Fargo drew into the cover of two big oaks and watched Ted and Robin pass. He stayed until they were almost out of sight. Ted was leading the way in a very long, wide circle, he noted as he moved out from the oaks.

Fargo rode slowly forward to see what had sent the youth racing back. He had the answer in minutes as he spied the first of two groups of Indians, perhaps a thousand yards separating them. He faded against another big oak and watched the Indians slowly go southward. Six to eight men headed each group, followed by a dozen women pulling four or five travois piled high with furs and tent canvas. Eight or nine near-naked kids came up last, pulling the tent poles with them. Fargo waited till the second group passed him. They were moving slowly and it took the better part of an hour for both groups to pass from sight.

Fargo turned and picked up the wagon tracks. The youth had led Robin into the low hills, up a half-dozen steep inclines, and had continued in his wide circle. Fargo followed, and almost three hours had passed before Maxwell returned to the flat land below. The Trailsman grimaced. The land had changed character, with low wide ruts almost miniature ravines, and Fargo watched Ted lead Robin along one. He continued to hang back, but he did more than watch the wagon ahead.

Habit made his gaze sweep the ground as he rode, and he slowed at two crossing trails of unshod Indian ponies. Ted Maxwell hadn't picked them up. He'd have stopped in instant alarm if he had, not aware that the tracks were a day old. Fargo moved on and later picked up a wrist band. "Assiniboin," he grunted aloud, and tossed it aside. The miniature ravines rose, flattened out, and became a wide plateau that stretched out for perhaps another hour's ride. Suddenly Fargo saw the wide expanse of flowers beyond Ted Maxwell and the wagon. The young man rode on and waved Robin to follow. Fargo's eyes narrowed as he peered at the flowers, a beautiful vibrant orange spotted with brown dots, narrow petals that turned in on themselves, all clinging to a dark-green stalk.

"Shit," Fargo exploded, and sent the Ovaro into a gallop. He was shouting, calling out to them as he raced forward, but he saw Ted Maxwell's mare already halted and the front end of the big Owensboro into the lovely flowers. It was starting to sink down, front end first, as the horses floundered and snorted in panic. Ted and Robin both turned to look at him as he raced to a halt and whirled the Ovaro in a tight circle. He yelled at Ted Maxwell first. "Get off your horse and put your lariat around his neck," he said, and waited while the youth complied. He sank up to his ankles when he touched the ground. "Now unhitch the brace. That'll stop them from pulling and sinking in deeper," Fargo said, and as the youth took sucking steps to unhitch the horses at the forward part of their shafts, Robin leaned forward to undo the rear harness gear.

The horses calmed at once but they were now knee-deep in the mire. Holding the lariat in one hand, the young man pulled himself forward, each step a sucking sound as he finally reached firm ground. Fargo whirled his own lariat and watched the noose fall over the brown mare's neck, let it settle almost into her brisket before he pulled it tight. Ted had halted alongside him and Fargo moved the Ovaro a dozen yards from him as he nodded to the brown mare. "Start pulling," he ordered. "Nice and easy, work with her."

The youth began to pull his lariat as Fargo tightened the pressure on his own, held the rope in place, and then pulled hard when the mare made an effort to free herself from the clinging ooze. It took nearly a half-hour, but the mare finally reached the firm ground and, again with the help of the lariats, pulled herself free.

Fargo lifted his lariat from the horse and Ted did the same with his. "The wagon horses next," Fargo said, and sent the rope spinning through the air to land over the neck of the nearest horse. Ted Maxwell did the same with his lariat, but this time he swung onto the mare. "Same as last time. Easy, go with the horse, don't try to pull it out until it makes an effort," Fargo said.

The first of the two horses reacted quickly the moment the lariats landed around it. It heaved its body forward in an effort to move in the oozing mire. Fargo and the youth pulled and pulled again at once as the horse tried another half-leap. Younger and more powerful than the mare, the team horse fought harder, and they pulled it free in less time than they'd taken with the mare.

The second wagon horse proved more difficult as it floundered more and dug itself deeper; the deeper it went, the more panicked it became. Only when it grew exhausted did it begin to stop thrashing and pull itself in one direction. But perhaps five minutes separated each effort and almost an hour passed before it was finally brought onto firm land, where it stood with its powerful chest drawing in great gasps of air.

"The wagon now," Fargo said, and secured his lariat to the left side of the axle while Ted put his at the right. "We pull together or this won't work," Fargo said. "I'll count to three." He counted and at "three" he moved the Ovaro backward. He watched the lariat, one end wrapped around his saddle horn, grow taut, and he heard the creak of it as it tightened to the breaking point. He felt the Ovaro's powerful hindquarters strain and cursed Robin for having such a goddamn big wagon. The mare was no match for the Ovaro's power, but she added just enough and Fargo saw the wagon's rear wheels slowly begin to turn. The front wheels lifted out of the ooze with a slurping sound and, once freed, rolled easily enough. Robin swung to the ground.

Fargo dismounted, took his lariat from the axle, and faced Ted Maxwell and Robin as he straightened up. "Don't you know what those flowers are?" he asked the youth. Ted shrugged and looked helpless. "They're Turk's-cap lily," Fargo said. "They grow in swamps and wet meadows. When you see a wide stretch of them like this, you damn well know it's a swamp." He put the rope on the lariat strap. "If you'd gone another six feet farther, you'd never have gotten out."

"Thank God you were here," Robin said. "I guess luck's running my way."

"Guess so," Fargo said, and turned to the young man. "You spent the whole afternoon going in a big circle for no reason."

"There sure was a reason. Indians, two groups of them," Ted said, finding a little bravado to put in his voice.

"I saw them. Squaws and kids pulling travois with a few braves riding along. They weren't war parties. Not even hunting parties. They were Chippewas on what they call the long walk . . . south to escape the worst of the winter. You wasted three hours when there was no need for it," Fargo said. He saw Robin look at the youth, who shrugged unhappily. "Go home, sonny, before you make a mistake you won't live to tell about," Fargo said, his voice gentler than his words.

"Wait a moment," Robin interrupted. "Where does that leave me?"

"I'll take you to Lakeside. Maybe you can find an experienced trail guide there," Fargo said.

"Can I go along?" Ted asked. "Maybe you could teach me some things. Or I could just learn by watching you. I'd like to become a trailsman. I was wrong to take on Robin, I know that. Uncle Tim insisted."

"I figured that," Fargo said, and turned Ted's request in his mind. He didn't see any harm in it, he concluded. "All right with me," he said, and shot a glance at Robin, who shrugged her agreement.

"You don't have to pay me," Ted said to her.

"Looks as though you get a free ride, honey," Fargo commented, and led the way to a low, wide-branched red ash to bed down. The tree looked over the flowers that hid the swamp beneath as the dusk began to fade.

"They're so beautiful. They make everything look so inviting and all the while they're really dangerous," Robin said.

"Sort of like a woman," Fargo remarked, and drew a quick glare.

Darkness fell and Ted Maxwell went off by himself. Fargo took down his bedroll and found Robin standing beside him.

"It wasn't just my good luck that you happened by, not with everything you saw," she said.

"All right, I followed you," Fargo admitted. "The kid didn't exactly fill me with confidence."

She stepped closer and searched his face with her robin's-egg-blue eyes. "How can you be so wonderful and so impossible?" she murmured.

"Practice," he said.

She reached up and her lips touched his, the soft smoothness again, but she pulled back as quickly as before. "That's for the wonderful part," she said, and disappeared into the wagon.

He stared after her for a moment. No promise in the fleeting kiss. No hint of something more. Nor had there been in the first time a few days back. Pristine little kisses, yet lips that were sensuously smooth. A very determined young woman in some ways, a naïve little girl in others, he decided. Maybe the two would never really come together. But maybe they would. Whoever was around her then might be very lucky, he mused. He crawled into his bedroll, unwilling to imagine further when it would bring only frustration.

4

The day came in brisk and Fargo led the way directly east. Ted Maxwell rode with him for the most part and he showed the youth how to use the creatures of the air and the land as signposts. "You need water? Watch the birds," he instructed. "They fly to water in the mornings and away from water in the evenings." He slowed when he saw a herd of deer across a field. "Always watch deer. They can tell you a damn bookful of information. When they're moving easy, there's nothing around. When they're nervous, something's making them that way. Could be a cougar, but it could also be a passel of braves you can't see yet. When quail suddenly scatter, you know something caused it. You stop, look, wait. When you trail, you learn to use everything around you."

They came to a wide stream and he showed Ted how to cross without leaving tracks by finding a flat rock and staying in the stream until one found another rock on the other side. "The Sioux have a method. They'll run their ponies back and forth along the very edge of a stream or river until they leave so many tracks you can't see where they crossed into the water. When they come out on the other side, they do the same thing," he said. He pointed out how to follow a moisture trail in the soil to find water and how the turning of leaves can presage rain and why the hoofprints of unshod

Indian ponies vanish much more quickly than those of a horse wearing shoes.

With it all, he managed to maintain a steady pace, and when the time came to bed down, everyone was ready to sleep at once. In the morning, the air remained brisk and he saw Robin had thrown a shawl over her shoulders. "It's very nice of you to take the time you're taking with Ted," she said over a breakfast of wild plums and hazelnuts.

"Turns the clock back. Makes me feel young again remembering the time I was learning," he told her.

When they moved on again he kept the steady pace and the land changed character to become low hills with thick covers of bigtooth aspen and mountain ash. It was midday when Fargo saw the soaring forms slowly wheeling in the sky just over a hill to their right. Robin pulled to a halt as she saw them, and his own feelings were mirrored in the combination of despair and anger in her eyes.

"No, please not again," she murmured.

"You two wait here," he said, and left them in a fast canter. He climbed the hill, crested the top, and went down the other side as he flung curses into the wind. Four wagons this time, he counted as he drew to a halt at the scene. The attack hadn't been more than a day ago, he determined. Assiniboin again, he grunted. They had streamed from the thick aspen just beyond the wagons, another ambush where the wagons had no chance to form a defense. He swung from the saddle, walked slowly from wagon to wagon, and chased away a half-dozen bold buzzards. He slowed as he spotted the prints of a lone horse wearing shoes. They moved from behind the last wagon and into the trees. He dropped to one knee to examine the prints.

He carefully pressed the edges of the hoofprints

with his fingers, then flattened his palms into the center of the prints. The tracks were a shade older than the unshod Indian pony prints, he decided— Perhaps only twelve hours older, but nonetheless older. The rider had left the night before the attack. Fargo frowned. He followed the hoofprints into the aspen, where they remained clear, and he hurried back to the Ovaro. He climbed into the saddle, his face drawn tight, and he rode back to where he'd left Robin and Ted.

She gave voice to the question in her eyes. "Him again?" she asked.

"The signs are there," Fargo answered. "But there are tracks I can follow this time. I'm going to do it."

"What happened to Lakeside?" she asked, a tiny smile touching her lips.

"No change. I'm just going to satisfy my curiosity," he said, and kept his face impassive. It was a half-truth, he muttered silently, and he knew she realized as much. He turned to the youth and pointed to the top of a high hill that became a ridge and continued eastward. "You get the wagon up there. It'll be hard going but you can do it. When you're there, stay in the trees and go east."

"When will you be back?" Robin asked.

"I don't know. I could run out of good tracks quickly, or I could be a day. I'll pick you up when I'm ready," Fargo said. "You just stay in the high tree cover."

"Yes, sir." Ted nodded. He moved away a dozen yards as he peered up at the high tree line and Robin's hand reached out to touch Fargo's arm.

"Be careful," she said, her face grave.

"Count on it." He took another moment to admire the strength and classic beauty of her face before he rode away at a fast trot.

He retraced steps to the wagons and followed the

hoofprints into the trees. They stayed in the trees, following a leisurely line. The horse had walked slowly—no deep marks were dug into the forest floor. The horse and rider had finally left the trees to ride along in the open, and Fargo followed, his eyes pausing to sweep the terrain on all sides. After another mile or so, the tracks turned into a deep forest of red ash, and Fargo followed as they wove through the trees.

He slowed suddenly, not because the tracks grew faint. They remained clear enough, but his nostrils drew in the scent of smoke, permeated with the odor of cooking. He was able to pick out deer, berries, and camas root, and he cast an eye up through the tree branches. Gray dusk was fast descending. He moved the Ovaro forward alongside the hoofprints. The odor of cooking grew stronger and then he heard the murmured sounds of voices. It was growing dark quickly and Fargo dismounted and began to follow the hoofprints on foot, the pinto tagging along a few steps behind.

Fargo didn't worry about their picking up his scent. The strength of the cooking odors prevented that, and he halted as the camp came into sight through the trees. He draped the pinto's reins over a low branch and went on by himself. The hoofprints led straight to the camp. He dropped to one knee as he came within a hundred yards of the camp. No hunting party campsite, he saw, but a main camp with squaws, kids, hide-drying racks, tepees and a longhouse at one end. The cooking fires were burning high, preventing him from seeing much of anything except the figures that moved about as the squaws began to cut meat from a wooden spit over the main fire. But he glimpsed a round-chested figure emerge from one of the tepees and the others part way for him. He wore only a breechclout, a white eagle's feather in his braided black hair, and an amulet of stone around his neck.

He was served the meat and vegetables by two squaws, and the others sat respectfully at a distance from him. He was clearly the chief, and when he finished and rose, Fargo's gaze followed the round-chested figure as the man disappeared into a tepee. Fargo saw the decorations on the canvas alongside the entrance flap. Assiniboin, he murmured to himself. The trail of hoofprints were proof enough themselves, yet there were things he had to see for himself, to prove beyond all doubt.

But he'd have to wait for night when the camp slept. He'd have to enter and look for things he couldn't see from where he waited. It'd be risky, but there were no sentries posted. They felt safe and secure and they'd sleep soundly.

Fargo settled down against a tree and relaxed as he considered what he had to do. The lone rider had come into the camp this way, but there'd been no other hoofprints. He'd left by another route, and Fargo's lips drew back in a grimace. He wanted to find that route and follow the tracks, and that meant waiting till daybreak.

He swore softly. That'd be cutting it pretty damn thin. That meant he'd have to be inside the camp when dawn broke and begin to examine the perimeter with the first gray light. How long would he have before someone woke and saw him? Thirty seconds? Two minutes? A half-hour? The question hung in front of him, grimly unanswerable.

He took another long, sweeping glance at the camp, his eyes moving along the oblong perimeter. He'd settle for ten minutes, he told himself. It was possible, he speculated. There was a fifty-fifty chance no one would wake with the first crack of dawn. He'd have to go with the odds, like it or not.

He sat back and let himself doze as the hours went by and the Indian camp grew still.

He let himself continue to doze, waking in between to watch the moon slide down the sky. It had reached the far edge when he finally rose and scanned the camp. Many of the braves were inside tepees, and most all the squaws and children. But there were at least a dozen figures asleep on the ground around the now-smoldering fires. Fargo moved forward on steps soundless as that of a mountain cat, skirted the edge of the camp, and entered through the deep shadows between two tepees. He moved past a snoring figure, circled another, and in a crouch, continued across the center of the camp.

He moved with careful deliberateness, his eyes searching through the darkness, peering past the hide-drying racks. He crept forward and dropped to one knee as a nearby figure turned, stayed asleep, and turned back again. Fargo moved on, spotted a dark mound some eight or nine feet in length against a distant tepee, and crept toward it. He cast a glance skyward and saw the first distant hint of grayness on the horizon, and he hurried forward, again skirted sleeping forms. When he reached the dark mound, he saw dried skins and blankets spread on top. He carefully pulled the top layer off and stared down at the long mound of clothing, boots and coats and stacks of rifles, a few dresses and bonnets, all of it taken from the ambushed wagon trains.

They were saving their bounty for the long winter, the clothing and blankets to wear, the rifles to use to hunt. Fargo's mouth became a thin line. These were the ones who sprang the ambushes, and the trail guide, whatever his name, had come here to their camp after the last attack. He'd probably done the same after every attack. Why? What terrible, ugly bargain in blood had been struck? Fargo pushed aside further wondering. There was no time for speculating about motives, not as the first pink-gray streaks appeared in the sky to herald the break of day.

He put the hides back over the blood bounty. If the Assiniboin found their loot disturbed, they could well ride out to comb the forest, and he didn't want that. Dropping to his hands and knees as the dawn grew brighter, he crawled to the edge of the camp, where he straightened into a crouch. His eyes sweeping the ground with every step, he began to make his way around the perimeter of the encampment. He felt his stomach tighten with every moment as the dawn came with malicious speed. He was some six feet from the edge of a tepee when he saw the hoofprints cross the edge of the camp and move into the trees. Two horses, one shod, the other an unshod Indian pony. He stared, frowned down at the prints, the unshod ones following the others. Two riders? he questioned. No, he decided as his eyes followed the prints. The second horse too close and following too steadily. One rider and a pony as a packhorse.

He marked the spot where the prints disappeared from his sight in the trees, between a big ash with a low bough bent almost at right angles and a pair of smaller entwined trees. He started to turn to make his way back to where he had left the Ovaro when he felt the hairs on the back of his neck stiffen. He turned to see an Indian standing not more than six feet from him, staring at him with a frown of surprise. The Assiniboin had plainly just stepped from the tepee, and wore only a thin thong holding his loincloth. He held a tomahawk in one hand.

Fargo used the moment of mutual surprise to reach up his trouser cuff to the double-edged throwing knife in the calf holster around his leg. He had the knife in his hand, just pulled below the edge of his trouser leg, when the Indian exploded out of his surprise with a leaping lunge, the tomahawk raised over his head. Fargo threw his knife without moving, a quick, upward flip of the wrist. The thin blade shot forward in a flat, upward trajectory, too fast for the other man to see in the dim dawn light. It hurtled into the base of his throat as he was lunging forward. His mouth fell open but no sound came from it as the force of his lunge carried him forward; he pitched to the ground facedown, his body twitching for a moment. Then he lay still.

Fargo's eyes went to the camp. No one had seen. It was still a place more asleep than awake, though he glimpsed other figures stirring. He retrieved the blade, wiped it clean on the grass, and continued on his way to where he'd left the Ovaro. When he reached the horse, he stayed in the trees, away from the very edge of the camp as he moved along the outside perimeter. Figures were on their feet now, and more were rising, stretching, starting to stir about. He came to the place he'd marked in his mind, the big ash with the strangely bent bough, and he halted to pick up the hoofprints again. Aware of the risk, he scanned the forest floor with his lips drawn back. But the newly awake in the camp were still only half-alert, their olfactory senses still foggy with sleep, and he was able to take another few dangerous minutes until he spied the prints.

He continued to lead the Ovaro behind him when he found the prints and followed in their trail. He only climbed into the saddle when he was well out of sight of the camp. The Assiniboin would find the slain brave any moment, he knew. They'd send out search parties at once. But they'd be racing around aimlessly. Yet he'd have to stay alert and be careful.

Fargo put the pinto into a trot as the prints stayed fairly clear and continued to move northeast. The rider and his packhorse had moved at a slow, casual pace, the prints showed, and Fargo followed up an incline as the land rose. He guessed he'd been trailing for another fifteen minutes when he heard the sound from behind, horses moving through the low forest underbrush.

He pulled to a halt at once. The Assiniboin had found their slain brother. Fargo scanned the trees ahead, spied a thick cluster of shagbark hickory, and moved toward it. He rode the Ovaro into the dense growth and dismounted, hurried into the clear again, and looked back. The horse was thoroughly hidden in the hickory, and as he moved farther away, he spotted the first rider, then saw a half-dozen more appear. They were spread out as they moved through the forest. Fargo dropped to one knee behind a six-foot-high stand of pokeberry. He watched the Assiniboin as they moved slowly, halting every dozen or so feet to scan the forest before they moved forward again.

One passed a dozen feet or so behind him, and then he saw another coming toward him. The Indian would pass within a foot of where he hid. He dropped to his stomach and held his breath. He could see the Indian's pony's legs slowly move past him, halt, and then go on again, and he allowed himself a deep breath. He pushed back onto one knee as the searching party moved on. Fargo let his ears become his eyes as he followed their path by the sound of their movements through the brush. Only when he heard them turn westward and finally move out of earshot did he rise to his feet and return to where he'd left the Ovaro in the hickory stand.

The Assiniboin search party was only one of probably three or four, the Trailsman knew, each exploring a different part of the forest. They'd go back to their camp when they decided the killer had gotten away, and that'd be the end of it. Fargo waited another ten minutes or so and then pulled himself onto the Ovaro and set out to follow the hoofprints once again. The path continued to lead upward, the land rising gently yet very definitely.

It was almost an hour later when he heard the sound before he saw its source, the unmistakable hissing roar of white water. He came into sight of the rushing rapids soon after, the water to his left, spitting and leaping as it raced over its rock-strewn path. He peered ahead, but the tree cover was thick and the rapids stretched onward deep through the forest. But there was a falls somewhere ahead, pulling the rushing torrent of water on its inexorable path.

The hoofprints stayed on ground a little higher than the rushing rapids, but they paralleled the water. The incline finally leveled off and began to turn downward. The white water still raced along below to his left, but he concentrated on peering ahead as he rode, his eyes searching through the trees. He'd gone perhaps another mile, he estimated, when he glimpsed the cabin, hidden away amid the trees and not more than a hundred feet from where the racing rapids took a turn to the right. Fargo reined to a halt and dropped to the ground on the balls of his feet. He walked forward, left the Ovaro with its reins draped over a low branch, and moved toward the cabin, each step a careful, cautious movement. He was grateful that the rapids would cover the sound of a twig cracking unexpectedly underfoot.

When he halted, the cabin was directly in front of him. His eyes narrowed, the big Colt in his hand, he surveyed the cabin. He detected no sign of activity, no wisp of smoke from the short stone chimney, no sounds from inside. Moving sideways, he circled the cabin and halted when he reached the rear. A single horse grazed on a long tether, short-legged, looked like an Indian pony. He moved on, finished circling the cabin, and when he did, he was satisfied there was no one inside. He walked back to where the horse grazed, lifted a foreleg to see that it was indeed the unshod Indian pony that had been the packhorse. He hurried back to the front of the cabin, opened the door, but the Colt was raised to fire, just in case he'd made a mistake.

He hadn't: the large single room was a silent place. He stepped inside. An open wood cabinet held a few dishes and cooking utensils. Extra clothing hung on wall pegs and a log bedstead occupied one corner of the room opposite the fireplace. But it was the other side of the room that made his eyes grow wide. One entire wall was almost invisible because of the piles of pelts that rose six feet in height. He saw beaver, fox, raccoon, wolf, ermine, weasel, hare, otter, even black bear. They were not the fruit of a single trapper's work, not even over a period of years. It was plain that they were the pelts the Assiniboin had gathered, and they were worth a fortune on the trading market.

Fargo felt the terrible truth pull at him, a sickening realization that made him shudder. This was the bargain written in blood. Money for lives. Pelts for human beings. A bargain conceived in hell, the fortune in pelts payment for leading the wagon trains to their deaths. To the Assiniboin, the pelts were cheap payment for having the hated white settlers led into their hands. To the elusive trail guide it was a way to riches without working for it, a fortune in pelts he could never amass on his own without years of trapping. But, above all else, it was a hideous bargain that could only have been made by a twisted, sick mind, a man completely and ruthlessly amoral, without any regard for human life. "A monster," Robin had called him. She had been more right than she knew.

His real name remained a secret. But Wade Barnum or Wayne Dumont, or whoever he was, had begun to take on form and shape. He had a reason now for his dammed deeds, a motive for his descent into hell. It was the oldest motive of all: greed. And he had a place where he kept his blood bounty. His ways had taken shape now. He left the wagon trains before the attacks, some the night before, others only minutes before. He rode away while the murdering ambushes were done, and then, leisurely, perhaps even the next day, he made his way to the Assiniboin encampment for his bloodstained payment.

That explained the packhorse, Fargo grunted. It had carried his pelts back to the cabin. He could be caught, Fargo mused as he walked from the cabin and carefully closed the door. If he could be found again, he could be caught. His method and his pattern had shape now. But first he had to be found.

That'd be a matter of sheer luck, Fargo remembered telling Robin, an almost impossible task of visiting every town at the right moment. But perhaps he'd been wrong, Fargo reflected. It might not be that impossible. The Judas killer couldn't roam too far. He couldn't use the entire state for his dark deeds. He had to keep his operation near enough to the Assiniboin camp in order to keep contact with them. He had to let them know his route and choose the time and place for his next deadly delivery. And, of course, stay close enough to pick up the pelts.

Fargo's conclusions gathered strength as he walked to the Ovaro and climbed into the saddle. It would still take luck to catch up with the Judas killer, but not as much as he'd first thought now that he knew the pattern of the man's operation. Fargo's mouth was a grim line as he sent the Ovaro east through the forest. The pied piper from hell couldn't be left to go on with his tune of death. He could be caught, but it would require the same malevolent cleverness he exhibited. The decision had already formed itself inside Fargo as he rode. It hadn't taken a lot of inner debate. But that still left Robin. Deciding about her would be more difficult.

Maybe she'd come down with an attack of common sense, Fargo grunted inwardly. Ted wouldn't take her farther. The boy was smart enough to know his limitations. And honest enough to admit them. But then his head wasn't filled with dreams.

Fargo put the Ovaro into a slow trot through the forest and finally emerged onto the stretch of open land where he could see the high ridge. He climbed the slope and moved eastward along the tall trees, worked his way inside the tree cover, and picked up the wagon tracks.

Ted had followed his instructions and stayed inside the trees atop the long high ridge, the tracks of the wagon forming a snakelike pattern as Robin drove around trees and chose openings as they appeared.

The day was beginning to slip into dusk when Fargo spotted the wagon ahead as he moved through the trees. It was halted and Fargo's eyes narrowed as he searched to see Robin or Ted. But he saw neither, and he reined to a halt, a sudden stab of unease in the pit of his stomach. He leaned forward in the saddle as his glance swept the trees around the big Owensboro again. No one came into sight. Nothing moved. Only the silent wagon met his gaze.

Fargo slid from the saddle and the Colt was in his

hand as he moved forward. Something was wrong, the feeling in the pit of his stomach told him. He reached the wagon on careful steps and the oath froze in his throat as he saw the figure lying face-down near the front wheels of the Owensboro.

He ran forward to drop to one knee beside the young man's still form and saw the two bullet holes in his back. Fargo pressed a hand against the side of Ted Maxwell's neck, but the search for a pulse was in vain. He rose, stepped to the rear of the Owensboro, and peered inside. All the cargo Robin had loaded into the wagon was there, but nothing else. He whirled and his eyes swept the ground, quickly picking up the hoofprints mixed in with boot marks. Four horses at least. Maybe more. The prints were too mixed together to tell. But the riders had clearly taken Robin with them.

The youth's body had been warm to the touch. He'd been killed not more than a half-hour ago. Fargo whistled and the Ovaro trotted up to where he waited beside the wagon. He swung onto the horse, his eyes on the hoofprints that trailed down the side of the slope. Dusk was moving in quickly and he sent the pinto into a trot as he followed the trail of hoofprints down the slope and onto the level land at the bottom. The trail stayed in tree cover and led west. They were moving in a straight line now as the trees thinned and Fargo continued on after darkness fell. He guessed he'd not gone more than another quarter-mile when he saw the faint, flickering shafts of a fire just beginning to burn.

He veered toward it as it quickly became a small orange glow, and as he neared the flames, he saw the shadowy figures moving around the edges of the fire. His searching eyes quickly found Robin. She was on the ground to one side, a lariat around her waist held by one of the men. Six in all, Fargo counted.

As he watched, one of them, tall and narrow-shouldered, with a prominent nose, took the lariat from around Robin's waist and yanked her closer to the fire.

"Get over here and warm yourself, sweetie," he said. "It turned real cold and we made this fire for you." He laughed, a snarling sound.

Fargo had moved a few paces closer and he saw the icy disdain in Robin's face as she stared back at the man. "How considerate. Real gentlemen, you are," she said.

"That's right. Hell, we could've had you back at the wagon, but we thought it wasn't right to do next to that young feller's corpse," the big-nosed one said.

"You didn't do it there because you were afraid somebody would be coming along," Robin corrected.

"Well, you told us somebody was coming after you," the man said. "Only you thought that'd make us turn and hightail it."

Fargo saw the admission in the angry glare Robin threw back. "Murderers," she hissed.

"As for the fire, it really is for you. We don't like riding a cold ass," the man said, and they all joined in the laughter.

"Who gets her first?" one of the others asked.

"We'll cut cards. High man goes first," the large-nosed one said.

Fargo saw Robin swallow hard and the fear come into her face. He slid from the horse and surveyed the scene again. Three of the men were standing close to one another, two more a few feet away, and the one holding Robin was alone, his back to the fire. Six, a formidable number. But Fargo had two advantages: surprise and speed. He carefully pulled the big Sharps from the saddle case. He'd need the steady accuracy of the rifle for the first shot. One of the men drew a deck of cards from

73

his jacket as Fargo raised the rifle to his shoulder. He aimed, brought the man's head in line with the front sight of the rifle, gently squeezed the trigger, and the big Sharps shattered the darkness with an explosion of sound.

He saw the man's head vanish in a cascade of bone and blood, but he was already swinging the rifle around. His next two shots slammed into two of the three men clustered together. The first one flew backward as the deck of cards scattered into the air. The man beside him collapsed face-forward. The third of the three tried to whirl and draw his gun, but he only managed a strange little dance as Fargo's shot slammed into his abdomen.

Fargo glimpsed Robin as she flung herself to the ground and rolled. He let the rifle drop as he drew his six-gun. The last two men tried to fling themselves to the side. Fargo's shot caught one in midair as he dived and the man's body executed a quivering jackknife and dropped to the ground with a dull thud.

The last one was running, but he was still outlined by the fire. Fargo's shot caught him in the spine and he toppled sideways into the flames. His scream lasted but a brief instant, and the little fire sent out a shower of sparks as it immediately began to die out. Fargo stepped out of the trees and saw Robin regaining her feet. She rushed toward him and fell against him, her head burying into his chest, her trembling silence needing no words. Finally she pulled back, shock still in her face as she met his frown.

"What the hell happened? You've a regular talent for getting into the hands of drifters and other rattlesnakes," Fargo said.

"We came onto them on the high ridge. They were ahead of us, looking down across the land below," Robin said.

"Probably looking for a stage to rob," Fargo said.

"I told Ted we'd best stop and stay back, but he said he was sure they were all right. Because you hadn't come back yet, he was anxious to get directions to Lakeside. He thought they could probably give them to us," Robin explained. "So we went on to where they were. They were surprised to see the wagon that high up on the ridge. Ted started to talk to them when they just shot him in cold blood. I couldn't move. I was frozen. Not just from surprise. From shock, I guess. Then they took me with them."

"Damn," Fargo said. "Not Ted's fault. He thought he was doing right. He hadn't the experience to be careful."

"My fault. I shouldn't have hired him on in the first place," Robin said.

"My fault, too, then. I left two babes out in the woods. And poor Ted Maxwell paid the price for everybody's mistakes. Somebody always pays."

Robin fell silent for a spell as they rode up the slope in the darkness. Her question came as they neared the top of the ridge. "Did you find anything?" she asked.

"Yes," he said, and told her everything he'd done and all he had discovered.

"My God," she breathed when he finished. "You were right about it."

"And I'm still without proof," Fargo said.

"You followed his trail to the Assiniboin camp."

"He can say I was following somebody else's hoofprints," Fargo answered.

"And you saw the pelts. You followed the trail back to his cabin."

"I didn't see him get them. He can say he bought them from the Assiniboin," Fargo countered. "I know the truth of it. I can put the pieces together. But, as I told you, knowing isn't proof."

"Then how can he be stopped?" Robin frowned.

"First, get lucky and find him. Then nail him red-handed," Fargo said.

"That'll be impossible."

"Hard but not impossible."

Robin shot a sidelong glance at him as she half-turned in the saddle. "You saying you're going to try?"

"Maybe. After I finish my visit to Lakeside," Fargo said.

"Seems you've had a change of heart," Robin said with a trace of waspishness.

"No. I can see a chance now where I couldn't before. That's the difference," he told her. "I'm not like some folks who go chasing after things when there's no chance to win."

She let a soft hiss escape her lips but said nothing more. They reached the top of the ridge and the Owensboro took shape, a dark bulk in the strong moon that had come up. Halting beside the wagon, Robin slid to the ground and stared at the silent form nearby and Fargo heard the half-sob come from her.

"Start collecting stones and small branches," he said as he dismounted. "I've no shovel, but the boy deserves a proper burial."

Robin nodded and hurried off to begin gathering the things needed.

Fargo carried Ted Maxwell to a spot between two big hickories and built a funeral bower of stones and branches. It was tight and secure when he finished and stepped back. "I'm not much on last words," he said, and Robin stepped forward.

"Let me. It's my place," she murmured. "The Lord giveth and the Lord taketh away. There must be a special place for the young and the good. I know Ted Maxwell will rest in peace in that place. Amen.''

She turned away and he saw the moonlight touch the wetness of her cheeks as she climbed onto the wagon. He rode beside her and stayed on the high ridge. They'd gone almost a mile before she spoke again. "This is such a cruel land," she murmured. "Cruel, ruthless, sick people."

"That kind make the biggest impression. You pass by the good, steady people, but they are there," Fargo told her. "But it's not only people who can be cruel. The land can kill, too. Nature has no pity for the weak or the foolish."

"Meaning me, of course. One of the foolish," she said.

"Your words, honey," Fargo said, and she fell silent again.

He rode for another mile and estimated there were only a few hours of the night left. He found an arbor shaded by the widespread branches of box elder and reined to a halt.

"Time to get some sleep," he said, and Robin's nod held grateful agreement in it.

The cold of the night was helped by the small fire he built; he set his bedroll beside it and she set her blanket near him and the fire and fell asleep in minutes. Ted Maxwell's death had reached her with a vicious cruelty. She'd had a sobering, shaking realization. Maybe that much good would come out of the youth's killing. One death preventing another. It had happened before. Maybe it'd happen again.

He closed his eyes and slept.

5

He let himself sleep into the morning sun, and when he woke, he saw Robin still hard asleep. He slipped on trousers, boots, and gun belt as his ears caught the faint sound of softly running water. He found a stream some fifty yards on. He made use of the cold, clear water and sat in a patch of sun long enough to dry off.

Robin was awake when he returned and the apprehension faded from her face as she saw him.

"Go down the slope west. You'll find a stream," he said, and she gathered her things and hurried off.

When she returned, she fed the horses and he leaned against the gray-brown, thin-fissured bark of the box elder as he watched her. "You know, don't you, that you can't carry enough oats to feed two horses through the winter?" he remarked.

"I'm going to let my trail guide take one horse back with him. I'll have enough to keep the other," she said.

He nodded, drew a deep sigh as he climbed onto the pinto. "You won't have to worry about keeping the other horse through the winter unless you've also planned on how to keep the wolves from him," he said.

She blinked back as he saw the moment of shock go through her. "Experienced woodsmen have survived the winters. You said so yourself. How do they keep their horses safe?"

"If there's no stable attached to the cabin, they build a closed lean-to," Fargo said.

"Then that's what I'll have to do," she said, and he shook his head at her airy confidence.

He rode ahead, far enough to survey the land yet keep the wagon in sight. He'd been given general directions to reach Lakeside long ago, and he'd followed them as best he could. He found a passage for the Owensboro to go downhill and waved Robin forward. He rode down to the gentle land below and led the way eastward through clustered pockets of red ash. He kept a steady pace, a dozen yards ahead of the wagon, and it was midafternoon when he saw the buildings of Lakeside appear. He slowed, let Robin catch up to him, and the town grew closer, more sprawling than most towns. A large lake spread out on the other side of the town, not more than a hundred yards on, Fargo estimated.

A fair number of freight wagons lined the main street as they reached the town, along with plenty of pack mules and a few heavy dead-axle drays used for hauling ore. The town had some ore wagon business, some haulage, but mostly it was the trappers with their mules carrying everything from furs to gold nuggets.

Fargo rode slowly alongside Robin as he searched the stores that lined the main street.

"I was informed there's a good inn. You can put your horses in the public stable," Fargo said.

"Will you be staying at the inn?" Robin asked.

"Might well be," Fargo said.

"I'll be staying only until I can get a trail guide," Robin said, and he ignored the reproach in her tone. He'd gone another hundred yards when he saw the store he'd been seeking, the wood sign over the door emblazoned with gold-paint letters: VERA'S VARIETY STORE.

Fargo drew the Ovaro to the hitching rail in front

of the store and swung to the ground. "Catch up to you later, honey," he tossed back.

"Wait. Why are you stopping here?" Robin asked.

"Because this is why I've come to Lakeside," Fargo said, and strode toward the store.

Behind him, a frown wreathing her face, Robin braked the wagon and climbed to the ground as Fargo disappeared into the store.

Inside, Fargo halted, one sweeping glance taking in the well-stocked shelves of fabric, dresses, sewing materials, baskets, jeans, boots, and a hundred other items.

The woman behind the counter looked up, deep-brown eyes focusing on Fargo, staring. He smiled and saw the wide, genial face explode in a shriek of delight. Her heavy, pillowy breasts bouncing under a tan blouse, Vera Conroy raced around the end of the counter to fly into Fargo's arms. "I'm dreaming. I don't believe it," she said.

"Believe it." He laughed. "I told you one of these days."

Vera's mouth was on his, open at once, pressing with instantly ravenous wanting. "Oh, God. Oh, God," she murmured. "I never let myself believe it, not even after your last letter." Her lips, full and soft, evoked instant responses and a flood of memories, all good, and Fargo felt the pillowed softness of her breasts pressing into his chest. She pulled back, more to catch her breath than anything else and Fargo's eyes surveyed Vera Conroy again. She had to be pushing thirty-five now, he realized, and she'd added some ten pounds. But Vera had always been a large girl and she carried it evenly, no sudden bulges, her broad face always more warmly pleasant than pretty, yet carrying its own undeniable attractiveness.

He saw Vera's eyes go past his shoulder and he turned to see Robin in the doorway, a furrow on her brow as she stared at him. "I thought you went on to find the inn," he said.

"I got curious," Robin said coldly.

"Vera, this is Robin Carr. I brought her into Lakeside with me. She was supposed to be part of a wagon train and she's lucky she wasn't," Fargo said. "Robin needs to find a trail guide to take her into the north country, all the way up beyond Upper Red Lake."

"You're wanting somebody to take you in the spring," Vera said.

"No, right now," Fargo said, and he knew Robin caught the combination of astonishment and incomprehension that flooded Vera's face. "Any ideas where she can put up a sign?" Fargo asked the older woman.

"She can put one up here in my place. Most folks stop by here. Then I'd put another on the stable wall outside and one more at Mike Smith's gun shop," Vera said.

"Thank you very much. I'll take your advice," Robin said. It was plain she was having a hard time being polite as she spun and hurried out of the shop.

"What's under her saddle?" Vera asked Fargo.

"Hopes and fears, dreams and disappointments," Fargo said.

"Hell, we've all had to wrestle with those things," Vera said, and hugged Fargo to her again. "You haven't changed one damn bit," she said, her eyes sweeping over him.

"And you're looking great, too," he said.

"All of a sudden I'm feeling young again with you here. All of a sudden the clock's turned back," Vera said. "But things are different now. I'm a respectable woman here in Lakeside. Carved a new life out for myself. I want to keep it that way."

"You tell me I came all this way just to talk?"

Fargo laughed and she pulled him to her, her mouth on his again for a long moment.

"No, God, no. I'm saying we have to be discreet. No saying to hell with them, the way we once did." Vera laughed. Her laugh, deep and sensuous, filled the shop, as warm and rich as he remembered it.

"Spell out discreet, honey," Fargo said.

Vera pulled back and went around to the other side of the counter as two women entered, both middle-aged, well-dressed, with pleasant faces.

"Hello, Vera," the taller of the two said from under a flowered bonnet.

"Hello, Mrs. Fullam. Hello, Sarah," Vera answered. "Come to get your knitting yarn? I have it all wrapped."

"That's right, Vera," the flowered bonnet said, and both women cast a glance at the big man with the handsomely chiseled face.

"This is Skye Fargo, an old and dear friend come to visit," Vera introduced. "Mrs. Fullam and her sister, Sarah, Fargo."

Fargo gave both ladies a wide smile. "My pleasure," he said, and both women returned the smile.

"We've a nice town here, Mr. Fargo. Perhaps you'll stay awhile," the taller woman said.

"Perhaps." Fargo nodded with another embracing smile and both women left the store with a touch of coquettishness.

"Haven't lost your touch," Vera said when the door closed. "Agnes and Sarah head the women's council in town. They're nice enough, but they're sharp-eyed."

"You were going to spell out discreet," Fargo reminded her.

"You take a room at the inn. That's for appearances' sake. Then you come spend the night. I live right here behind the shop," Vera said.

"Expect me soon as it gets dark," Fargo said.

Vera came around the counter and hugged him to her again.

He left then as the first signs of dusk appeared. He walked the Ovaro down the street to the public stable, where he gave orders to curry the horse during the night. He had just registered into the white clapboard Lakeside Inn and received his key when he saw Robin striding down the ground-floor corridor toward him, fury in the robin's-egg-blue eyes.

"So that's your idea of an important meeting," she hissed. "An old girl friend, a night in the sack?"

"I was thinking more like a week," Fargo said blandly.

Blue fury flew from her eyes. "Night, week, month, it's disgraceful. You turn your back on helping me so you can exercise your loins? It's disgusting. And it's unfair. It shows what kind of person you really are."

"Aren't you forgetting something, honey?" he asked, interrupting her bitter tirade.

"Such as?" she snapped.

"Such as I told you why I won't help you. Vera has nothing to do with that," he said.

"That's what you say."

"And that's what I mean," Fargo said, letting his voice grow hard. "Now, you go nurse your feelings and sulk and maybe come to your senses." He turned from her, found the room at the end of the corridor, and went inside, aware she stared after him.

The room was small but neat, a large double bed taking up most of it, a single window letting in the last of the dusk. He lay down, stretched sideways across the bed, and thought about Robin. She had lashed out at him partly out of fear, he realized. She knew time was slipping away from her and she still had no trail guide. She feared losing the dream by default, and that made his intransigence that much more maddening. But he'd hold out no understanding to her. Understanding would breed hope, at the least encouragement, and he'd give her none of either.

He closed his eyes and catnapped as night fell, and after it had been dark for an hour, he rose, slipped from the room, and hurried from the inn. He walked through the town in the deepest shadows against the buildings until he reached the shop. He saw the light on behind the shop and moved around to see another doorway with two steps leading up to it. He knocked softly; the door was opened in moments and he saw Vera in a full-length white satin nightdress.

Memories rushed through Fargo's mind. Of course, Vera had been almost ten years younger then, but the years hadn't dimmed the simple, direct sensuality of her, a glowing, throbbing force. She turned, no words, only the message in her eyes, and led the way into a bedroom, simply decorated, a small lamp on low providing a soft glow.

She sat down on the edge of the bed, a small smile on her lips, unsaid waiting in her eyes. He took off his gun belt and shirt and saw her eyes glisten with appreciation of the muscled symmetry of his torso. He hurried, shedding the rest of his clothes, and as he did, Vera crossed her arms and pulled the nightgown from her shoulders, a quick motion that let it fall to her waist. The pillowy breasts still thrust out with strength and firmness, Fargo saw, each rounded fullness topped by a large, brown-pink circle and its flat-topped little tip. Vera leaned back on her elbows and the rest of the nightgown slid away and he saw the rounded little belly, the extra few pounds only emphasizing the earthy throbbing of her. Beneath it, the very thick, very dense black nap, a distinguishing feature he'd always remembered about Vera. She raised her arms as he came to her, pulled him against enveloping softness with an almost angry force.

That, too, had always been a part of Vera, a pure, driving wanting, no games, no coy hesitations, and her mouth on his was instant proof nothing had changed. Her tongue darted out, explored, sought and he drank in its stimulating touch. Her hands came up to close around his face and pull him down into the pillowy breasts.

"Oh, oh, God," Vera groaned as his mouth found first one brown-pink tip and then another, pulling, sucking, drawing in the softness that surrounded each until he felt the flat-topped nipple against the roof of his mouth. She groaned and sighed at once and her hands were moving along his back, pressing hard into his buttocks while he continued to pull and caress her breasts. "Jesus, oh, yes, Jesus, yes," he heard her cry out, and she arched her back to press the white mounds further into his mouth.

He drew his lips from one throbbing nipple to trace a simmering line down her body with his tongue. Vera's ample hips turned, writhed, half-rose as he moved across her belly, pausing to circle the tiny indentation. His hand moved down, pressed along the inside on one full thigh and then the other, felt the warmth of her skin as her own hands clutched at him. He spread his fingers as he pushed slowly through the very thick, deep-black nap, felt its wiry strands curl around his fingertips and, just below, the soft rise of her pubic mound.

He slid his hand downward, to the inside of her thighs again where they met the end of the thick, dense V, and found her skin wet. Vera was flowing with desire and he heard her groan as he pressed. "Oh, oh, aaaaaah, please, please, oh, come on, come on, Fargo," she cried out, and his hand slid along the wet skin of her inner thigh, cupped tight against the soft portal.

Vera cried out as her hands dug into his back.

He touched, stroking the sweet, moist lips, and Vera's voice rose higher, her legs kicked outward, twitching and twisting.

Her hands were pulling at him, digging into his buttocks to bring him over her, and he let himself go, brought his warm, pulsating organ against the damp, dark portal, and plunged in deeply, the path made easy by her wonderful wetness. "Oh, Jesus, aaaaaiiiiii . . ." Vera screamed as her torso rose, lifted, pumped, each motion a vigorous, wild explosion, her full thighs clasping around his waist. She pulled his face down against the heavy, soft breasts as sounds of half-screamed groans came from deep inside her.

He pressed his face deep between the pillowy mounds, turned to take half-bites out of first one, then the other, and all the while Vera pumped and twisted and pumped. He felt himself being carried away on the waves of wild desire, flesh infusing flesh, touch unto touch, skin unto skin, and the senses totally and irrevocably in command.

Vera's wild pumping suddenly halted and her back arched; he felt the spasms go through her. "Oh, now, oh, God, now, now, yes, yes . . . oh, now," she cried out, and he let himself erupt with her as she fell back onto the bed with him, arms, legs, thighs wrapped around him, each a soft vise of ecstasy. He clung to the climax with her, that moment when all feeling, all thinking, all existing is capsuled into one brief instant. When she suddenly grew limp and the despairing groan rose from her, he lay atop her, stayed in her as he rested his head against one pillowed mound.

He lay quietly with her for a long moment, not pulling away until the sweet embers had died down. He came to lay beside her and she turned on her side and let one deep breast fall against his cheek, the flat-topped tip almost touching his lips.

"Been a long time, hasn't it?" he said gently.

"Too long," Vera murmured.

"Why?" he asked.

"Nobody came along to make me want to," she said with simple honesty. "Not often enough, anyway."

"I'm sorry," he said.

"Don't be," Vera answered. "I'm not. Wonderful memories are better than meaningless moments." She rose onto her elbows to lay half over him, one hand smoothing the hair from his forehead, her smile, as always, warm and guileless. "And now you've come to make the memories come alive again. I'm not asking for more. How long can you stay, Fargo?"

"I don't think I can be discreet for more than a week," he said, and her deep, throaty laugh came at once.

"I don't know that I could either, not with you," Vera said. "And my life here is important to me. I guess I'll have to settle for a week."

"Unless I can find new ways of being discreet," Fargo said.

"Meanwhile, the night is still young," Vera said, and he felt her hand close around him. Slowly, she began to stroke and caress, and he could feel her wanting stir at once, gathering itself for the sweet explosion she sought. He let her enjoy her caressing, felt himself stirring again as she brought her lips to him with soft, sucking kisses, and finally, more quickly than he'd expected, he was making love to her again. The room became a world within a world, a private place of private ecstasies, and once again Vera's groaning screams rose to a climax of pleasure and the thick black triangle was moist as it pressed hard against him until the screams turned to silent sighs and he lay still with her.

"Who says you can't turn the clock back?" Fargo commented.

"Not I." Vera smiled as she turned and lay half across him, her deep breasts soft against his chest, the warmth of her flesh a soothing contact. It was a time he always enjoyed, tender touchings, pleasure without the turmoil of passion, the sweet embers of afterward.

He and Vera had lain quietly together for perhaps a half-hour with murmured words of lazy reminiscences and were drifting off to sleep when the quiet was shattered by the sharp knock at the door.

"What in hell?" Vera said as she sat up, deep breasts swaying from side to side.

The knocking persisted, sharp, quick rappings, as Vera rose, pulled a bathrobe around herself, and strode from the room. She'd left the bedroom door ajar and Fargo could hear clearly as she opened the rear door. He sat up and swore as he heard Robin's voice. "I have to see Fargo," she said.

"What in hell makes you think he's here, girl?" he heard Vera bristle.

"He wasn't in his room at the inn. I assumed he'd be here," Robin said, a touch of disapproval in her voice.

"You've got your nerve assuming that," Vera shot back with righteous anger, and Fargo smiled to himself.

"I just thought . . ." Robin said, words trailing off as she melted under Vera's anger.

"Well, you can just think yourself out of here," Vera said, and Fargo heard the door slam shut. He was resting on one elbow when Vera returned to the room, a frown still creasing her face. "You give her any cause to come looking here for you?" she asked.

"No, but she knows you're the reason I came to Lakeside," Fargo said. "She just took it from there, reasonably enough."

"Too much so. I don't want her talking out aloud about us," Vera said.

"I'll see she doesn't," Fargo said as Vera shed the robe and brought her full-figured body down to lie against him. "She's a good sort bent on letting her dreams destroy her," he said.

"I've seen that before," Vera said as she burrowed down against him and drew a deep, contented sigh before she fell asleep.

Fargo stayed, let himself sleep with her, and woke before the dawn prepared to light the new day. Vera murmured protest in her sleep as he left, dressed, and she was hard asleep again when he went out the back door. He paused outside, the town still dark and silent and hurried back to the inn. The desk clerk's chair was empty and Fargo hurried down the corridor to his room, started to fold one hand around the doorknob when he saw that the door was open. Only a crack open, but nonetheless open.

He drew the Colt, remembering that he hadn't locked the door, seeing as how he was using the room only for propriety's sake. Lakeside hadn't seemed a town for dry-gulchers and petty thieves, yet he knew that their kind roamed freely, sometimes choosing the most unlikely towns. He pressed the door open slowly, the Colt raised as he went into a crouch, and his eyes were narrowed as he peered into the dark room. He saw the darker bulk of someone on the bed and he straightened up, crossed the room in three quick, long-legged strides, and the dark bulk became a person, half-covered by the sheet.

"Wrong room, mister, whoever you are," Fargo growled, and pressed the barrel of the big Colt into the shape under the blanket. The shape half-turned and he caught the tumble of flaxen hair, silverish in the dark of the room. "For Christ's sake," he hissed as Robin pushed out from under the blanket and blinked at him. She was fully dressed, he saw as the first gray light of dawn began to filter in through the window.

"I fell asleep," she said, rubbing a hand across her eyes.

"What the hell are you doing here?" he snapped.

"Waiting for you," she answered. "I went to your friend's place. She said you weren't there," Robin muttered, and he saw her cast a sideways glance at him that was made of suspicion. "I came back here to wait."

"Why didn't you wait in your room until morning?"

"I wanted to see you the minute you came back. I didn't think you'd be out all night," she said reproachfully. "Where have you been?"

"That's none of your damn business, honey," Fargo tossed back. "Now, you want to tell me why you had to wait in my room? Hell, you could've been shot."

Robin's face grew instantly grave. "He's here," she said.

"Who's here?" Fargo frowned.

"Wade Barnum or Wayne Dumont. He's here, in Lakeside," Robin said, and swung from the bed as the dawn grew brighter inside the room.

"You sure?" Fargo frowned.

"Yes, I saw him and followed him. He went into the saloon and I looked in through the window. It's him. He even has that damn vest on. This is your chance. You can get him now before he goes on somewhere else and you lose him."

"Get him for what?" Fargo asked.

"You know for what, dammit," she flung back.

"I know, but I also know I've no proof of anything. I can't drag him to the sheriff without proof. We've been through this."

"You can't just let him get away."

"I don't expect to do that. If you're right, if he's here, I'll tail him if I have to," Fargo said.

"I'm right," Robin said.

Fargo's thoughts tumbled wildly as he stared into space. Plans began to form of themselves, only rough outlines now. He'd need more time to sort and think things through. The Judas killer was clever. He wasn't a man to bring down with slipshod, unformed, and hasty actions.

"You get on to your room. Nothing's going to happen right away and you can catch a few hours' more sleep," he told Robin.

"What are you going to do?"

"Think some," he said.

"I'll walk through town all morning until I see him again," Robin said. "I think you should come with me."

"No," Fargo said, more harshly than he'd intended. "The one thing I don't want to do is make him suspicious. You put up your notices and let me find out a few things before you go looking for him again. I'll meet you here at noon."

She frowned for a moment. "All right, I do have to get those notices up."

He went to the door with her and watched as she walked to the first room at the head of the corridor. He closed his door and stretched out across the bed, his thoughts tumbling through his mind again. He closed his eyes, let plans present themselves and fall aside for one or another reason. When the sun was fully out, the morning come fully around, one plan remained. He rose and shed clothes to wash with the water from the big metal basin in a corner of the room. He shaved and dressed again, and the plan stayed formed, the only one that could work.

But he'd need help. He'd talk to Vera about that when the time came. First he had to find out if the Judas killer was merely passing through Lakeside or marking time. He left the inn, stopped in at the stable to check on the Ovaro. The horse had been well-curried and Fargo decided to let him enjoy the good oats he was getting for a little longer. He walked back through town and reached Vera's shop.

She had opened and a man and two women came out with packages in their arms as he entered. Vera's smile was quietly smug. "Your little friend was here, not more than ten minutes ago," Vera said, and pointed to the notice posted against the wall near the door. "She apologized for disturbing me last night. Or maybe she was still fishing. I'm not sure."

Fargo smiled. "I know why she was trying to chase me down last night," he said. "It's a long story. I'll tell you later. Right now I need some information."

"Whatever I can," Vera said.

"Is there a wagon train leaving Lakeside soon?" Fargo asked.

"Indeed there is. A few days from now, I think. Folks have been coming in to pick up extra clothes," Vera said. "Two wagons are due to arrive today, I hear. Most are folks from outside, but there are two wagons of folks from town who want to go west."

"They have a trail guide?"

"Yes, a very handsome young man."

"You know his name?"

"Walter Hobbs," Vera said. "He brought four people in to buy some extra winter boots." Fargo's eyes grew narrow and Vera picked up his change of mood at once. "What is it?" she asked.

"Part of that long story," Fargo said. "I didn't see any wagons gathering in town."

"They're just outside the north end of town."

"Thanks. Think I'll take a walk out there."

"What's this all about, Fargo?" Vera questioned with a frown.

"Tell you later," he said, and started for the door

as her questioning stare followed. He went outside and walked toward the north end of town. He'd almost reached it, the six wagons in sight, when he saw the big Owensboro roll up to him. "Damn, what're you doing here?" he hissed.

"Just driving around, getting some supplies," Robin said airily.

"And looking for Barnum or Dumont or whatever."

"He's there, with the wagons."

"His name's Walter Hobbs," Fargo told her.

"It's him," Robin said.

"Now, you drive yourself back over by the warehouse and stay there," he said, nodding toward a low, long building.

She made a face but wheeled the wagon around and drove toward the shed.

He walked on to where the line of six wagons waited, most of them Conestogas, a few canvas-topped rack-bed rigs. Men, women, and children were gathered in clusters alongside the wagons, some fixing gear, others shifting belongings inside the Conestogas. Fargo saw the tall, handsome man talking to a handful of people, and he paused as he came to the wagons. "You the trail guide?" he asked.

"That's right. Walter Hobbs," the man said, and Fargo took in wide shoulders, a good, compact frame, and the reddish hair hanging loosely atop a face that was rakishly handsome. Only a hint of cruelty around his mouth marred his good looks. It was a feature few would notice, Fargo realized.

"When are you heading out?" Fargo asked.

"Maybe tomorrow. Maybe the next day. Soon," the man said. "Why? Want to come along?"

"No, but I rode in yesterday and passed a wagon on its way here. They were looking to hook up with a train," Fargo said.

"If they get here in time, they're welcome to join," Walter Hobbs said expansively. He flashed a warm smile at two of the women nearby. Fargo's eyes went to the leather vest the man wore over a checkered shirt, the letter W stitched over the right-hand breast pocket.

"That's right good of you. Many trains won't take on latecomers," Fargo said.

"I say the more the better," Walter Hobbs answered. "There's safety in numbers."

"There is," Fargo agreed.

"I didn't get your name, mister," the younger man said.

"Fargo, Skye Fargo."

"You change your mind and want to join, you just let me know, Fargo," Walter Hobbs said with another expansive smile.

Fargo nodded, backed away a few paces, and watched as Hobbs took the reins of a gray horse and began to lead the animal from the wagons. The man walked toward a water trough near the long shed and Fargo strolled a few paces behind and swore silently as he saw Robin at the trough with the two horses from her wagon. Still cursing under his breath, Fargo slowed as Walter Hobbs halted at the trough with his horse. The man peered at Robin, Fargo saw, and he saw Robin look up and meet the man's eyes.

"Well, if it isn't Mr. Wade Barnum," she said, acid wrapped around each word. The man continued to stare at her. "I was supposed to leave with the other wagons from Colepoint. I had a broken axle, remember, and you wouldn't wait," Robin said.

The man offered a smooth smile. "Sorry, you have me mixed up with someone else. We've never met and my name's Walter Hobbs," he said, keeping his voice blandly pleasant.

"Really?" Robin said, and Fargo took a half-dozen long strides as he walked past the trough.

She glanced at him as he passed and saw the fury in his eyes, though he didn't look at her.

"That's right," he heard the man say as he walked on. "You've made a mistake, little lady."

"Maybe," Fargo heard Robin answer, her voice tight.

He glanced back to see her start to climb onto the Owensboro. He slowed his pace to a saunter as Walter Hobbs rode by, and he kept his casual stride. He heard the Owensboro coming up behind him a few moments later. Hobbs had gone out of sight but he could have turned into one of the side alleyways. The wagon came alongside him and Fargo strolled on.

"Get your ass to the inn," he rasped without turning his head. Robin drove on and he continued to saunter through town until he finally arrived at the inn and saw the wagon drawn up alongside. She wasn't with it and he strode into the inn and saw her waiting in the doorway of her room. "Goddammit, I told you to stay out of sight," he roared.

"How was I to know he was going to stop at the water trough?"

"Being at the water trough isn't staying out of sight," Fargo shouted as he went into the room and slammed the door shut. "You may just have blown my chance to get him," he accused. "He knows you recognized him."

"That doesn't mean I know anything about what happened," Robin said.

"No, it doesn't. That's the one saving grace. He probably figures that you got someone to bring you out here and that you don't know what happened to the rest of the wagon train from Colepoint. I think he'd have reacted more strongly if he thought you knew," Fargo said. "But I'll know that later."

"How?"

"If he comes back. If he doesn't, it means he

thinks you know and he's on his way to Wyoming or Texas."

"I'm sorry."

Fargo ignored her apology. "You stay out of the way. The less he sees of you, the better. I don't want him getting nervous. You stay here and wait for replies to your notices," he told her.

"All right," she agreed with a trace of sullenness. "But I'm not going to be shut off from everything. You have some kind of plan, I know it. I want to know what's going on."

"You'll know when the time comes for knowing," he said.

She searched the chiseled stone of his face and knew she'd learn no more then.

Fargo strode from the room and felt her eyes following him down through the lobby and out into the street. He hurried to Vera's and saw the curiosity come into her eyes at his questions. "You've got a sheriff here, I take it," he said.

"Yes, Tom Draper," she answered.

"What's he like?"

"He's good, careful and cautious but a no-nonsense man. You want to tell me what's going on?" she questioned.

"Tonight," he said, and hurried from the shop. He found the sheriff's office set back a few yards from the main street and two men in the outside room as he entered. One wore a sheriff's star pinned to his shirt, the other a deputy's badge. The sheriff regarded Fargo out of gray eyes and a square face. Hair starting to turn gray, with perhaps twenty pounds too much on him, the man nonetheless gave the impression of solidity and patient strength. The deputy was younger by some twenty-five years, Fargo guessed, sandy-haired, with a smooth face that held more sincerity than strength.

"Yes, sir?" Sheriff Draper asked.

"The name's Fargo, Skye Fargo. Some call me the Trailsman," Fargo introduced himself.

"Sheriff Tom Draper. My deputy, Jack Ward," the man said. "I've heard of a man called the Trailsman. Not up in these parts, though."

"That's right. I don't usually get up this way," Fargo said. "I need some help."

"What kind of help?" Draper asked.

"First, I have to tell you a story you'll have a hard time believing," Fargo said. "But every word of it's true." He threw a glance at the deputy. "I want it kept between us," he said.

"Anything I hear, Jack hears," Sheriff Draper said.

"Whatever you say," Fargo said, and lowered himself onto a straight-backed chair as he began to tell what he had to say. He told it just as it happened: meeting Robin first, then the first massacred wagon train, and he took the rest as it came, the slow realization of the extent of the terrible deeds and what he had finally found at the cabin. "And he's here now, getting ready to take out another wagon train under another name, Walter Hobbs," Fargo finished.

The sheriff's expression had grown from interest to incredulousness and now he sat back, his brow creased. "Yes, I know about the wagons getting ready to move out. And I heard about the attack on the wagon train from Colepoint," Sheriff Draper said. "But this is the damnedest story I've ever heard." He paused, stared into space for a long moment. "I've seen men do a lot of real bad things but nothing like what you've been telling me. Frankly, Fargo, I find it hard to believe."

"You can believe it," Fargo said. "Every word of it."

"I'll be honest, friend. For me to believe a story like that I'd need some proof of who you are. Feller came in here once, said he was sheriff of Turner's

Point, had papers to prove it. Only we later found out he'd stolen them," Draper said.

Fargo frowned as he realized he hadn't anything with him that would prove who he was. "Why the hell would I make up a story like that?" he asked.

"If you were settling an old grudge with this Walter Hobbs feller that'd sure as hell do it," the sheriff answered. "You never did say what brought you here to Lakeside."

Fargo drew a bitter sigh. He hadn't wanted to bring out his reason for coming, but he had no choice. "Ask Vera Conroy," he said. "She'll vouch for me."

He saw the sheriff's eyebrows lift. "Go ask Vera to stop in, Jack," he said to the deputy, who left at once. "I know, you're thinking I'm being a pain in the ass," Sheriff Draper said to Fargo when they were alone.

Fargo smiled. "Something along those lines," he said.

"Look at it from my side. That's one hell of a story you're asking me to buy," the man said, and Fargo nodded.

"It is, and I don't blame you for being careful. Fact is, I'm glad to see that. It means you're the kind of man I'll be needing," Fargo said, and sat back to wait.

Deputy Ward returned with Vera in a few minutes, and she took in Fargo's apologetic shrug with a mixture of curiosity and surprise.

"The sheriff needs some proof I'm who I say I am," Fargo told her. "I'm sorry, but there was no one else to call on."

"Fargo, here, has told us one hell of a wild story, Vera," Draper said.

"He's the Trailsman, Tom. I've known Fargo for years, back before I came to Lakeside. Whatever he's told you, you can take as gospel," Vera said.

"That's more than good enough for me," Tom

said. "Vera's a fine woman and an asset to this town."

"Anything else?" Vera asked.

"No. Thanks for coming down, Vera," the sheriff said.

Fargo's quick glance at her held its own silent message and Vera hurried from the office.

"Tell me what you want, Fargo, and you'll get it," Sheriff Draper said, anger in his voice now.

"Can you get a posse of, say, thirty men who'll do what you tell them without asking questions?" Fargo asked.

"Yes," the sheriff said.

"Good. I don't want to bring him in and have some circuit judge say we don't have enough real proof he did all those things. I worked out a way to put an end to him you might call poetic justice. It won't do his Assiniboin friends much good, either."

"I'm with you all the way," Tom Draper said.

"He's been real clever, but he has a routine now and I'm going to turn that against him," Fargo said. "First, I want him watched twenty-four hours a day, but from a distance. We can't make him suspicious."

"I've another deputy besides Jack, here. We can put a watch on him," the sheriff said.

"If I'm right, he'll ride out for a night, maybe a day—for some advance scouting, he'll tell the others. But he'll really be making contact with the Assiniboin. The wagons will roll a day or two after he returns," Fargo said.

"What do we do then?" Tom Draper asked.

"I'll lay it out for you, step by step. It'll be cutting things close, but it can work," Fargo said.

"I'm listening," the sheriff said as he pulled up a chair.

6

Fargo had taken the time to go over everything twice, examining each detail for himself as well as for the sheriff. But finally he was finished and the plan was firmly set in everyone's mind. It was late afternoon when he left Draper and his deputy and strolled through town to where the six wagons were lined up. Some of the pioneers were just waiting, others still nailing sides on tighter and engaged in last-minute chores. He saw the reddish-haired man come toward him with an expansive smile. He was a smooth charmer, Fargo noted again with silent fury.

"Howdy, friend. That wagon you spoke about hasn't shown up," the man who now called himself Walter Hobbs said.

"Guess they decided not to stop in town," Fargo said. "You can't ever figure people."

"That's true," Hobbs said. "You going to join us?"

"Not likely. Going to visit awhile longer with an old friend here in town," Fargo answered. "But thanks for the offer," he added, offered a smile of his own, and strolled on. He felt the man's eyes on his back as he crossed to the other side of the street. Suspicion and distrust were part of the man, along with his twisted, sick ruthlessness, Fargo was certain, and he kept his pace casual.

The day was beginning to come to an end when

he reached the inn and started for his room. He hoped to put off meeting with Robin as long as possible, but the hope vanished as he saw the flaxen hair push out from the doorway to her room.

"Been waiting for you," she said, and he stepped into the room. "Where've you been all day?"

"Meeting with the sheriff. I'm going to need his help," Fargo said.

"You told him your plans?" Robin asked, and he nodded. She waited and her foot tapped on the floor as the questions hung in her eyes. "Well?" she snapped finally when he remained silent. "You going to let me in on them?"

Fargo grimaced inwardly before he answered. "No," he said, and braced for her stormy reaction. It came at once.

"What do you mean, no? You said you'd tell me." She frowned.

"I said when it was time for telling. This isn't it," Fargo corrected.

"When's that going to be? When it's over?" Robin shot back.

"Maybe."

"Dammit, this isn't fair. I was in this from the beginning. I found him here in town for you. I deserve to be in at the finish."

"Maybe you do, but it can't be that way."

"Why not, dammit?" she spit at him.

"If you'd stayed out of sight the way I told you to and not had such a big mouth when you faced him, maybe it'd be different," he flared. "But he knows you and I'm sure he's concerned about you. I don't know if he'll try to get to you, but I can't take that chance. If you don't know anything, you can't tell him anything."

"He won't come near me."

"I can't risk it," he said. "This is our chance to get him and I can't let anything get in the way.

Take your guide and get out of here. That's what you really want. Forget about this."

"I can't forget about this monster. Besides, nobody has answered the notices. I've no guide."

"It'll be a few days before he takes the wagons out. You may find someone by then," he told her. "This is your last chance."

"That's my worry," she snapped. "What are you going to be doing now?"

"Watching, waiting, staying on top of it," he told her. "Leave that to me and stay out of his sight."

She glowered from under deeply knit brows. "I'll think about it and get back to you," she said.

"You don't have to think about it or get back to me. Just do it," Fargo said, brushing past her as he left the room. The door slammed shut behind him.

In his room Fargo stretched out across the bed. She was hurting, he knew. Nothing was going right and she had to be aware that time was running out fast. But she was stubborn and headstrong and she hadn't listened to him.

He relaxed, let the night grow deeper, and finally made his way to Vera. "I'm sorry I had to call on you," he said, and her lips on his told him he was forgiven.

"What was that all about?" she asked, and he quickly told her and realized he grew angrier with each telling. "My God," Vera breathed when he finished. "There are a lot of lucky people waiting with those wagons who don't know it yet."

"I hope so," Fargo said, and her glance questioned. "Things can always go wrong."

Her arms slid around his neck and the deep breasts were soft mounds against his chest. "You'll make them go right when the time comes, and I'll make them go right here," she murmured, and in moments she was proving her words, naked with him on the bed, her breasts almost smothering his face and the deep thick nap pressed hard into his abdomen. Her hands sought his burgeoning strength, found it, and stroked and caressed, and then, falling onto her back, she brought him with her, not letting go until she had inserted his seeking warmth into her waiting, wanting wetness.

She was pushing up, arching her back at once, her feet planted flatly and firmly on the bed, and he felt himself lifted with her, then plunged downward as he came down and her soft, full-fleshed thighs clamped around him. Again there was no pretense with Vera, none of the spirit and none of the flesh, and he felt himself carried along by the pure power of her wanting. When her groaning cry of utter climax spiraled into the room, he heard his own voice joining with hers.

Later, as she lay quietly with him, her finger traced an abstract design along his chest. "Does all this mean I won't even have a week of being discreet?"

"Could be," he admitted. "I might have to move quickly."

"Then we'll have to make the most of whatever moments we have," she said, and once again turned the promise into reality.

She was hard asleep in the small hours before the dawn when he rose, dressed, and slipped out of the house. He had gone only a few dozen feet up the street toward the inn when he glimpsed the shape moving from the deep shadows. The Colt was in his hand and raised before he caught the tumble of yellow hair. "Goddamn," he swore as he dropped the gun into its holster. "You trying to get yourself shot?"

"So this is how you're keeping watch," Robin hissed, her eyes sparking blue flame. "I see what you're staying on top of, and it isn't Walter Hobbs."

"What in hell are you doing here? Spying on me?" Fargo returned angrily.

"I just wanted to see for myself," she said. "You were probably here the other night when I came looking for you."

"Maybe I've just been talking about old times."

"Hah," she snapped as she fell in step beside him.

"Not that it's any of your damn business," he shot back.

"You tell her about Hobbs and your plans?" Robin asked, and he heard the catch in her voice.

"About Hobbs. Nothing else. You know, you're sounding a lot like a jealous woman."

"Ridiculous," she snapped, too quickly. "I just don't like being tossed aside while you share your confidences with everybody else."

"We've been through this. I explained why I can't tell you anything. It's for your own damn good, too."

"I know, just like not taking me north is for my own good," she flung at him.

"That's right."

"Well, you don't have to worry so much about what's for my good. I can decide that," Robin said, and again he heard the catch in her voice. They had reached the inn. He halted, took her by the shoulders, turned her to face him, and saw her fighting to hold back the tears that edged her eyes.

"Sometimes, when nothing goes the way you want it, there's a reason," he said with firm gentleness. "The good Lord's trying to tell you something."

She didn't reply but her lower lip quivered and he led her to her room.

"It's not right, not helping someone just to go see an old girl friend," she muttered.

"Listen to me," Fargo said quietly. "Vera saved my life once, long ago. She hid me when I was hurt and four no-good killers were looking for me. We became more than friends, and when she moved here, I promised to come visit sometime. Only sometime never seemed to arrive, and then I finished a job downstate and decided to make sometime happen. I've never forgotten what she did for me."

Robin had fought back the tears and she blinked gravely as he fell silent. "You saying I'm ungrateful? You saved my life. Twice," she said.

"I'm saying you're so caught up in yourself you can't see straight," he said, growing harsh.

Her eyes hardened at once. "If I don't go north, I want in on catching this monster. I want something good to come out of all this."

"No," he said. "That's final."

"Then I'll go north on my own, guide or no guide!"

"Even you wouldn't be that dumb," he said. "Now, get some sleep." He stalked away from her and heard her slam into her room. He undressed and lay down on the bed, not at all certain she'd not carry through her threat. But he couldn't think about that. Or do much about it. His target had been chosen. There was no greater importance.

He rested some, let the morning come, and later made his way to the sheriff's office, where Tom Draper rose as he entered. "You were on the nose, Fargo. Hobbs rode out early this morning. Jack talked to some of the wagon people. Hobbs had told them he was going to do some advance scouting."

"He'll be back late tonight, I'd guess. You can call off your twenty-four-hour watch now. The rest will go pretty much as expected. We'll know when he pulls out with the wagons," Fargo said, and Sheriff Draper nodded agreement.

Fargo left and walked to the stable, where he

retrieved the Ovaro and saw Robin's big Owensboro resting alongside the rear of the stable. He took the Ovaro out of town to let him stretch his legs, and his eyes swept the terrain westward. Hobbs would take the wagons along a flat stretch and then between two lines of red ash where the land began to rise slowly. It was the logical path and he'd stay logical until he was at least a few days out of town.

It was late in the day when Fargo returned to Lakeside and went to the inn. Robin's door was closed, but he could almost feel the anger from behind it. He stayed in his room till night came and then made his way to Vera's, where she held him close at once. "One more night. I'm grateful for each one," she said, and proceeded to prove her words. When finally he slept beside her, he was satiated.

He left close to the break of day, rode the Ovaro back to the inn, tethered the horse to the side hitching post, and went to his room.

The bright morning sun and a knocking at the door woke him. He answered to find Tom Draper. The sheriff entered, his eyes bright with excitement. "He came back a few minutes ago."

"Which means he made his contact," Fargo said. "It also means he's been riding all day and most of the night. He'll need a day to rest. He won't be moving out till tomorrow at the earliest."

"We'll know when he does. A wagon train departing town always gets a send-off from the town folks," Draper said, and turned to the door. "I'll be hearing from you."

Fargo nodded. Alone again, the Trailsman washed, shaved, and dressed, and when he passed Robin's room, the door was closed. He paused at the desk clerk. "The young lady in Room One, she's been expecting some callers. Did she have any yesterday?" he asked.

"Nope. None this morning so far, either," the clerk said.

"You see her this morning?" Fargo asked.

"No," the man said, and Fargo walked from the inn. She was staying closed away, fighting with all the angers and disappointments inside her. Or maybe waiting for him to respond to her threat. He'd let her sulk, work it all out on her own. It was best that way.

He went outside to the Ovaro, unsaddled the horse, and gave his back a quick freshening with the body brush from his saddlebag. When he checked the horse's feet, he found a nail missing from the right forefoot shoe, so he walked him to the town blacksmith's, where he found two horses already waiting their turn. It was well past midday when he finally had the shoe fixed and rode past the line of wagons. He saw no sign of Hobbs and guessed the man was asleep nearby or in one of the wagons.

That evening, he went to Vera and found her waiting with only a robe on. "Another night. We're doing right well," she said. He nodded and decided not to tell her this might be their last night.

Vera made him almost forget about Judas killers and ambushes waiting to be sprung, innocent people being led to their deaths. It was growing harder to leave her full-figured beauty before dawn, he realized, but when the time came, he pushed himself from her and left as she stayed hard asleep. He rode back to the inn, unsaddled the Ovaro, and took the saddle into the room with him, where he caught a few hours more sleep.

When he rose and went outside, Robin's door was still tightly shut. He saddled the pinto and he'd just finished when he saw the sheriff hurrying up to him.

"They're getting ready to pull out; the women-folks are buying last-minute things," Tom Draper said.

Fargo's eyes narrowed at once. "I'll be staying plenty back. You stay a helluva lot farther and just follow my tracks the way we planned."

"I just hope we can do it. I'm no trailsman," Draper said. "We'll be starting out twelve hours after. I don't want to be following the wrong footprints."

"You won't. I bought a bag of salt. I'll leave a trail with my prints," Fargo said, and the sheriff nodded in relief. He was a conscientious man, Fargo realized. Tom Draper didn't want his mistakes to botch catching the vicious killer. "You'll be staying back, but you'll be catching up at the same time, don't forget that. The wagons will be moving slowly," Fargo said, and Tom Draper nodded again.

"See you soon enough," Tom said, and hurried away.

Fargo walked the Ovaro to Vera's shop and she looked up in surprise as he entered, but the surprise instantly turned to unhappy realization. She came to him at once, folding her arms around him.

"I'm glad for every night we had," she murmured.

"Likewise," he said. "I'm glad I came."

"It was wonderful. Only, now I want you back again sooner," Vera said.

"Might be," he said.

She kissed him tenderly. "Good luck, old friend," she said, and watched him leave from the door of the shop.

He rode slowly, passed near the wagons, and saw they were still waiting. He decided to ride from town to a cluster of box elder on a low hill that overlooked the road west. He faded himself and the Ovaro into the trees and waited, finally dismounted as the time dragged on. Hobbs still hadn't appeared with the wagon train. He had thought about Robin and now he had time to think again about her. He'd stop to see her for a moment before he set out to trail the wagons. He'd already decided that. A last try to talk some common sense into her. She deserved that much.

The day had almost come to an end, dusk laying itself over the land, when he saw the line of wagons slowly rumbling along the road west out of town. Hobbs had given himself almost the entire day to rest and now he'd only travel a few hours before making camp. That would give him another full night of rest.

Fargo felt the frown dig into his brow. Hobbs seemed to have done an unusual lot of hard riding, more than seemed needed. Had he gone to a more distant spot with the Assiniboin to choose the ambush site? It was possible, Fargo pondered, an exercise in caution.

He'd find out soon enough, Fargo knew as the line of wagons disappeared down the road and the dark descended. He'd be able to pick up the wagon tracks even under a weak moon.

He turned the Ovaro toward Lakeside. He rode into town, all the shops already closed, and drew to a halt at the inn. He dismounted and saw the desk clerk in the doorway. "You see the young lady in Room One today?" he called, and the man shook his head. Fargo brushed past him as he strode into the inn and halted at the door of Robin's room. He knocked, received no answer, put his ear to the door, and heard no sounds from inside.

He folded one big hand around the doorknob, turned, and the door opened. The room was empty.

He felt the instant grimness settling inside him as he went back to the Ovaro and rode to the stable. The big Owensboro was no longer alongside the stable wall near the rear, and Fargo's lips pressed hard against each other. "Damn-fool girl," he swore aloud as he put together what had happened. No one had answered her notices and he'd refused to take her into his confidence. Angry, hurt, and still fueled by dreams and determination, she had decided to go north on her own. She probably hoped to find help along the way someplace.

But he couldn't go chasing after her, not now. Bringing down the Judas killer came first. A wagon train of innocent men, women, and children came first. He let his thoughts wrestle with guesses about time. Robin had probably left a day ago. A night ago, he corrected himself. While he was with Vera. And bringing down Walter Hobbs could take at least three, maybe four days more. That would give her a good week's start. Enough, but not impossible to make up. She'd not be traveling fast with the big Owensboro. He'd return, pick up her trail, and go after her. He'd be able to catch up to her before she was too far into the north country. Damn-fool girl.

He put the pinto into a trot, left town, and followed the tracks of the wagon train in the pale moon. It was what he had to do, he knew, just as he knew he'd come back and go after Robin. The saving of innocent lives dictated the first. Compassion dictated the second. Were either really a matter of choice? he wondered as he rode up a slow incline after the wagon tracks.

7

He'd followed for perhaps three hours when he spotted the dark bulk of the wagons grouped together for the night. He turned the Ovaro up a hillside and into a stand of black oak. The night had turned cold. Winter was sending its unmistakable signals, but a fire was out of the question and he was grateful for the warmth of the bedroll.

He slept quickly and woke to a bright sun and a crisp morning. He could see the wagons and he watched them begin to roll again. He stayed back far enough so he could only glimpse the procession through the stands of oak and hickory.

Hobbs kept onto flat stretches wherever possible and chose the lowest hills to climb when the terrain made it necessary. To all appearances, he seemed a completely proper trail guide and Fargo was certain that all those in the wagons were satisfied with his competency. They had no way of knowing better.

Fargo felt his bitter anger at Hobbs grow sharper with each passing hour. The day drew to an end and again Fargo camped in the trees, on a hill that let him look down at the distant wagons.

The next morning repeated the one before as Fargo again hung back and followed. The terrain stayed reasonably passable and Hobbs rode on ahead of the wagons, disappearing for over an hour sometimes and returning again to lead the way into a shallow valley or around a blockade of rocky hills.

As dusk began to settle, the Trailsman climbed onto a ridge of land and followed from the top until Hobbs called a halt for the night. Fargo let his gaze sweep the terrain they had come through, his eyes narrowed in the dusk. He didn't want to see Tom Draper. That would mean the man was too close. But he estimated that the sheriff was not that far behind now. A small shower of fall leaves swirled around Fargo as he set out his bedroll. The night wind held a cutting sharpness.

He glimpsed the camp fires by the wagons until they were put out. He finished the cold beef jerky out of his saddlebag and welcomed sleep. He stayed atop the ridge when morning came and followed the line of wagons below. He glimpsed Hobbs moving back and forth alongside the wagons, pausing to exchange a few words with each family. He was playing his role of conscientious trail guide to the hilt, Fargo grimaced. The anger inside him had become ice. When dusk began to creep across the land, Fargo moved closer to the wagons.

This was the third night they had been traveling. Hobbs could be ready to make his move at any time now, Fargo realized, and as darkness fell he edged the pinto still closer. The camp fire was clear now, as were the figures that moved in its light. He could even pick out Hobbs. The man sat alone and stayed that way as the fires burned down and the others began to climb into and under their wagons. This was not the night, Fargo knew, and he settled himself into a thick cluster of high brush and slept until the morning dawned.

He woke with a certainty deep inside him. This night would begin the terrible deception. Hobbs had been traveling more than long enough. The time was drawing near and he swept the land behind with a quick glance. Habit more than anything else. But the sheriff had better be in position when the night came, Fargo muttered grimly. If he wasn't, it would all have been for nothing.

As the distant wagon train prepared to move on, Fargo searched the ground near where he'd camped for the night and finally came up with the long, dried-out stick he wanted. He secured it to the rifle case, climbed onto the Ovaro, and once again followed the wagons.

But the spiral of quiet excitement stayed with him and it helped make the day seem shorter. Hobbs contributed to that by pulling the wagons into a camp spot just as the first purple of dusk began to roll across the low hills. Fargo hurried the Ovaro forward, as close to the wagons as he dared, and then dismounted to edge closer on foot. Dropping to one knee, he could see Hobbs in a conference with four of the men from the wagons, gesturing into the distance. Fargo's eyes peered on and saw nothing except two long stands of shagbark hickory that faced each other along a low hill with a wide passage between them.

The twin lines of hickory were some two miles on, he estimated, and a bitter sound dropped from his lips. They were perfect for an ambush. He watched the small conference with Hobbs break up, the others return to their wagons, and Hobbs sit down by himself.

Dusk came, turned into the dark of night, and the cooking fire was lighted beside the wagons. Fargo retrieved the Ovaro, led the horse behind him as he moved closer to the camp in the blackness of the trees. He found a thicket of high brush under a tall black oak from where he could see the entire encampment. He settled down to wait. The night turned cold again and the meal was eaten quickly and the fire put out. Fargo watched the wagons grow still. The pale moon let him see Hobbs resting against the trunk of an oak.

Perhaps two hours passed, the wagons still, when Fargo saw Hobbs push to his feet. Watching, the icy excitement inside him stirring, the Trailsman saw the man go to his horse and climb into the saddle. Keeping the horse at a walk, Walter Hobbs moved out of the camp, turned along the far side of the wagons, and slowly disappeared into the trees. The Judas killer's hideous task had been completed. He was on his way to the cabin, unhurried, supremely confident. After all, practice makes perfect. In the morning, he'd take his Indian packhorse and casually make his way to the Assiniboin camp to collect his bloodstained wages.

"Only this time it'll be different, you murdering bastard," Fargo hissed aloud into the night, and he forced himself to wait another two hours. He had to be certain that Hobbs was well out of sight of the encampment. Finally he rose and took the long, dry stick from alongside the rifle case and crept to the wagons on silent steps. Halting at the nearest wagon, he knelt down and pushed himself under it to the rear axle. He took one end of the stick and smeared some of the axle grease on it. When he finished, he pushed his way from under the wagon and silently left the camp. He returned to the Ovaro and picked out an oak with branches made for climbing. He began to pull himself up into the tree, the long, dry stick in one hand, and he kept climbing until he was near the top. He halted, straddled one of the last of the wide branches, and used a lucifer to light the stick.

He pressed the match against the axle grease and watched the grease take fire at once. In moments one end of the dry stick was ablaze and he began to wave the makeshift torch back and forth, from one side to the other, each motion a slow half-arc.

Every dozen or so times he changed direction as he waved the torch, and he continued the slow, deliberate motion until the length of wood began to burn down near his hand. He had waved the torch for almost a half-hour, and when he could no longer hold on to it, he let it drop down through the tree and watched it hit the ground and go out in a last flurry of sparks against the dew-damp grass.

He pulled himself from the wide branch to a more comfortable perch in a crook of the tree and his eyes swept the dark forestland below. The pale moon was sliding toward the far end of the sky when he saw the dark shapes of the horsemen making their way through the trees, each one moving with slow caution. Fargo quickly climbed down the tree and was on the ground when the first horseman neared.

"Over here," he called softly, and saw Tom Draper wheel toward him.

"We were mostly guessing our way after your torch went out," the sheriff said.

"You guessed well," Fargo said. "Hobbs is gone. Pulled out a few hours back."

"Just as you expected he would," Tom Draper said. "Now let's wake the others."

"Carefully. Let them hear us. We don't want them shooting in panic," Fargo said, and led the way to the wagons. The sound of some thirty horsemen, even walking their mounts, quickly woke those inside the wagons and Fargo saw a half-dozen heads appear, a rifle just below each head.

"You can come out. You're all safe," Tom Draper called out, and Fargo heard a voice from one of the wagons.

"It's Sheriff Draper. By God, it's the sheriff," the voice called out, and other figures began to emerge from the wagons, many of the men still in their long johns.

"Bring out the women and children," the sheriff said, and soon the wagons were emptied, everyone staring at the visitors with apprehensive frowns.

"It's a long story, friends, and there isn't time for telling all the terrible parts of it," Sheriff Draper said as he addressed the settlers and then nodded to Fargo. "But thanks to this man, Skye Fargo, you're not going to ride into a massacre." A gasped murmur rose from the listeners. "That's right, friends," the sheriff went on. "That's what the man you knew as Walter Hobbs had arranged for you. He's not here, I know that."

"That's right. He told us he'd be riding out tonight because he wanted to be on a high ridge when dawn broke," one of the men said. "He told us to go on, come morning, and he'd meet us where two stands of hickory face each other."

The sheriff exchanged a grim glance with Fargo. "Just the way you called it," he said, and returned his eyes to those gathered in front of their wagons. "Now, it'll be daylight before the hour's up. I want you all to get dressed first. Then I want some of your more ample ladies to give us a half-dozen of your capes, dresses, and bonnets. You are all going to stay in the trees with our horses while we go on with your wagons. We're getting a surprise party ready."

"What happens to our wagons afterward?" one of the men asked.

"We'll be bringing them back to you," Tom Draper said. "And seeing as how you'll be without a trail guide, I'd suggest you all turn and go back to Lakeside with us till you can find somebody else."

"Sounds like we haven't much choice," another of the men muttered.

"This massacre business, are you sure you're right?" one of the women questioned. "I just can't believe that about that fine, handsome young man."

"Neither could the folks in the other four wagon trains," Fargo said. "At least, I only know about four. There are probably others that no one is ever going to hear about."

A heavy silence fell over the listeners and they slowly turned and went into their wagons. The sheriff had his men dismount, and the half-hour before dawn broke became a time of silent, grim activity. Just before the first pink-gray light of the new day tinted the horizon, Sheriff Draper led everyone from the wagons into the deep of the forest along with the horses his men had ridden.

When day came to streak the sky, growing quickly bright, the horses were hitched to the wagons and the wagon train began to move. Fargo rode alongside the lead wagon, where Tom Draper held the reins. Beside him a figure in a bonnet and a big cape sat quietly. The scene was duplicated on most of the wagons that followed, though two had only a driver. The canvas on each wagon had been untied along the sides where it was normally strapped to the top of the wagon frame. It was a detail that wouldn't be noticed by anyone more than a few feet away from the wagons.

Fargo's eyes stayed ahead and he rode with his body relaxed in the saddle as the wagons approached the twin stands of hickory. He spoke to Tom Draper without turning his head. "They'll come fast and hard, shooting the minute they clear the trees," he said. "There's not going to be a lot of time or room."

"The men have their orders. They're to open fire the minute the attack starts," the sheriff said as the wagon began to move between the two thick stands of hickory. The creak of the wagon wheels was the only sound that disturbed the silence, and Fargo rode with one hand on the butt of the Colt at his side. He kept his face facing forward, but his eyes flicked to the trees on each side. The lead wagon had reached the midway point in the passage when Fargo caught the movement of leaves at the hickory to his right.

"Here they come," he hissed, the words hardly out of his mouth when the trees erupted in the horde of near-naked, racing, whooping forms. They came with a flurry of arrows that whistled through the air and Fargo leapt from the Ovaro to land on both feet. He glimpsed Tom Draper rein to a halt and the bonneted figure beside him whip out a big Remington .44 and fire off a volley of shots before both men leapt to the ground. Fargo dropped as a hail of arrows slammed into the wagon inches from his head. He rolled beneath the wagon, spun, came up firing, and saw one of the attackers topple from his pony.

The air suddenly exploded in a thunderous barrage of rifle fire and Fargo could see down the line of wagons as the canvas was pulled up at the base and the rifles poked into the open. The Assiniboin recoiled as though they had smashed into an invisible wall, and Fargo saw at least a third of them fall from their ponies amid the vicious volley of gunfire from the wagons. He saw surprise and consternation sweep through the attackers. Instead of the few ineffectual shots from the surprised men, women, and children, they were hit by a barrage of deadly, accurate rifle fire from inside the wagons. The easy prey had suddenly become a formidable force. The hare had turned into a raging cougar.

Fargo drew a bead on one of the attackers, fired, and saw the Indian fly from his pony in a sideways arc. He saw at least four more Assiniboin go down, and he glimpsed the chief with the braided black hair and barrel chest. Still in the background, the chief frantically directed his warriors with hand signals, and the attackers quickly broke away from one another to become harder targets as they streaked away in all directions. Most made a wide circle to return to the chief.

Fargo saw the leader send his men to the attack again. This time they attacked from both ends of the passageway to avoid the direct rifle fire from the wagons. They also stayed spread out, and the return fire from the wagons was not as effective as before.

But the sheriff's men were good-enough marksmen and they took their toll of the attackers. When nearly a dozen more of his braves had fallen, the Assiniboin chief recalled his warriors, the stone amulet on his chest glinting in the sun. Fargo pushed himself out from beneath the wagon as the Assiniboin raced away to disappear into the trees. It was over. They had been hit hard, taken completely by surprise, the battle short but furious. They had never recovered from the surprise or the initial blow. They'd return to their camp, filled with fury. Maybe they'd return for their dead. Maybe not. In any case, he'd not be here to know.

He saw Tom Draper hurrying down the line of wagons, inquiring of the men in each, and the sheriff returned in moments. "Seven men wounded, none serious," he said. "That leaves Hobbs, and you're going after him."

Fargo nodded and called the Ovaro to him. "Thanks for your part," he said to Tom Draper with a handshake.

"You have trouble finding Hobbs, you come get me," the sheriff said and Fargo's smile held an icy anticipation.

"I'll find him. I know just where he'll be," he said, swung onto the pinto, and rode away with a final wave. He looked back to see the line of wagons slowly turning to return to their owners.

He turned the Ovaro northeast, climbed a low

hill covered with violet-blue harebell, and set a steady, ground-eating trot. When he'd ridden into the late afternoon and neared the Assiniboin main camp, he spotted the hoofprints of the unshod Indian ponies, riding hard into the camp.

They had probably been back for at least an hour, he guessed, and he slowed the pinto to a walk. He could almost feel the seething rage as he neared the camp. The Assiniboin chief would have concluded but one thing: Hobbs had betrayed him, sold him out for money. Rage and hate beyond bounds whirled through the Indian, Fargo knew. But the man wouldn't race off to find Hobbs. He'd fill in the rest of his betrayal as he saw it, certain that Hobbs, thinking he was killed with the rest of his warriors, would come to collect his pelts.

He was half-right, Fargo smiled grimly. Hobbs would come, but he'd come sublimely unaware of what had happened. He'd come to collect his blood pelts just as he did after every one of his Judas deliverances. But this time justice would be served, the best kind, poetic justice, where evil turns on itself. Fargo slowed as the Assiniboin camp was but a few thousand yards ahead through the heavy woodland. He risked riding on a little closer before he slid from the saddle and left the Ovaro out of sight in a thicket of fireweed around a large red ash. He moved forward on careful, silent steps, his eyes sweeping the trees. He found the path to the camp Hobbs had used before and he settled down behind the trunk of a wide hickory, confident that Hobbs would use the same approach.

The afternoon had begun to slide into dusk when he spied the movement through the trees, felt his muscles tighten as he saw the horse and rider take shape, the pony following behind. Fargo moved from behind the tree, darted silently to another as Hobbs drew closer. The man rode with casual confidence. Fargo felt the hatred rising through his body. Hobbs was almost in front of him when suddenly the sound filtered through the trees from the Indian camp, women's voices in a high, wailing call, undulating, growing soft and then loud again. He had heard it before, the women's lament for the dead, the wailing dirge common to all tribes.

Fargo saw Hobbs rein to a halt, a frown instant on his brow. He peered through the trees, listening as the wail sounded again. Suspicion shot through his face and Fargo cursed under his breath. Suspicion was built into the man, along with his twisted cunning. The Assiniboin chief had made a mistake in letting the women wail their lament. He probably didn't expect Hobbs would know its meaning. Perhaps he was half-right again. Perhaps Hobbs didn't know the meaning of it, but his alarm senses had been set off. Something was different than usual, the wailing sound one he'd not heard from the camp before. It was plainly not a sound of victory or triumph.

Fargo swore again inwardly as he saw the alarm wrap itself around Hobbs, the man's face instantly tight with apprehension. With his own sixth sense, he knew something was wrong. Ruled by cautious cunning, he started to turn his horse in a circle. Survival came before another shipment of pelts.

Fargo moved from behind the tree, darted forward, and Walter Hobbs turned in surprise, his hand going toward his gun. But the big Colt was in Fargo's hands and Hobbs saw the barrel pointed at his head.

"Don't even try," Fargo growled. Hobbs stared back, his eyes narrowed. "Take the gun out, two fingers," Fargo said. "Take it out and throw it into the bushes."

Hobbs hesitated and heard the click of the hammer being pulled back on the Colt. He carefully lifted his gun and tossed it away. "What the hell is all this about?" he growled.

"Now turn and ride, just the way you usually do," Fargo ordered.

Walter Hobbs stared back with his eyes growing still narrower. "What'd you do, goddamn you?" he questioned.

"Ride in, same as always," Fargo hissed.

"What'd you do?" Hobbs returned. He wasn't as fearful as he should be, Fargo frowned.

"Made sure you get what you deserve," Fargo said. "Now ride in or I'll blow you apart here."

"I'm not riding anywhere till you talk," Hobbs said, and there was a sudden bravura in the man's tone. Or perhaps he could put on a good act. Fargo frowned, unsure which it was. He drew the hammer back on the Colt again.

"There or here," he said.

"I wouldn't do that, Fargo," Hobbs said with something close to a sneer.

Fargo swore inwardly. Was Hobbs trying to bluff his way? The act could be just another side of the man's cunning. He met the half-sneer in the man's eyes and tried to see through it when suddenly he saw the movement of the leaves in the trees to his right. He threw himself flat on the ground and rolled into a thicket of tall brush, but he had a split second to see Hobbs turn in the saddle to glimpse the three Assiniboin coming through the trees. Lying on his stomach in the high brush, Fargo watched Hobbs try to wheel his horse in a tight circle and race away, but he was too late.

The three braves, running with the swiftness of wolves on the hunt, reached him. One leapt up, grabbed him around the waist, and yanked him from the saddle. Hobbs hit the ground hard and they were on him at once, pulling him to his feet.

Two held him by the arms while the other smashed a hand across his face.

"Son of a bitch," Hobbs yelled. "Get the hell away from me."

The Indian slapped him again and yelled at him in the Siouan language the majority of the plains tribes spoke. It was obvious that the chief was the only one Hobbs could communicate with. They started to drag him away and he resisted, and Fargo saw the man's eyes sweep the trees, fear in them now, yet an air of boldness still clinging to the man.

"Goddamn you, Fargo, I've got her," Hobbs screamed, and Fargo felt the coldness seize him at once. "That's right, Fargo, I've got her," Hobbs shouted into the trees. "I saw her that night outside the shop with you. I knew something was going on, so I came back the other night and took her." Fargo cursed silently. Of course, the night he'd thought Hobbs had gone to meet with the Assiniboin. He'd been drowned in Vera's body for the whole night.

"An ace in the hole, Fargo. I always keep an ace in the hole," Hobbs was screaming as the three Indians dragged him away, paying no heed to his wild shouting.

"You hear me, Fargo. She's got twenty-four hours, then she's dead. You get me out of this or she's dead, Fargo, dead," he was still shouting as he was dragged through the trees. "Twenty-four hours, Fargo, that's all she's got. You get me out or she's gone."

The Assiniboin dragged him on and Fargo heard his yelp of pain as one of the Indians smashed a blow into him. But Fargo wasn't listening any longer as he rose to one knee. Hobbs wasn't lying, attempting a last-minute piece of desperation. It all fit, all suddenly chillingly clear. An ace in the hole. That fit, too, basic to the man's diabolic twisted cunningness. Fargo took a moment to be grateful that he hadn't told Robin anything. She'd had nothing to reveal and so Hobbs had gone on as usual. Somehow, Fargo found it difficult to be thankful for small victories.

He felt his fingers digging into his palms as suddenly all his plans were shattered. The final victory would be one last triumph for Hobbs if he let it go on. Poetic justice was suddenly nothing more than a phrase. If he let things take their course, the victory would be as it was planned. But now Robin's life would be added to all those who had paid the price before her. It was her own fault, damn her, he swore. She had brought this moment about by waiting for him outside Vera's. All her own doing, her own suspicious stubbornness. Perhaps letting the Judas killer go free was too high a price, he grimaced.

"Damn her," he swore aloud as he pounded one fist into the ground. He had to try to save her. Logic and reason were sterile exercises for the mind. He had to somehow rescue the Judas killer. He had to spare the monster what he deserved. Conscience, feelings, emotions, they were too strong for mere reason and rationality. Fargo rose and began to move through the darkness that had blanketed the forest. As he neared the camp, he realized that only one thing gave him a chance to rescue Hobbs: they wouldn't kill him quickly. Only the brave deserved that. Hobbs was neither brave nor worthy. He was a betrayer. To the Assiniboin, he was the perfect candidate for torture and slow death.

Fargo saw the camp come into view through the trees, at least three fires burning to afford ample light. He crept closer. Some of the women were still wailing, but the sound was softer now as they huddled to one side. He found Hobbs, already stripped naked and tied to a stake driven into the

124

ground. The Assiniboin chief and a half-dozen of his remaining braves looked at their captive from a dozen feet away. At a signal from the chief, a line of squaws began to move toward Hobbs. Each carried a switch in her hand, and doing a little dance at the same time, they began to beat Hobbs. Short blows first, then longer, harder, and Fargo saw Hobbs' skin turning red with welts. Soon Hobbs was uttering a short, gasped curse of pain with each blow.

They beat him with the switches for over an hour, pausing to rest, then returning to their pleasure, and Hobbs was now covered with red welts from his neck to his ankles. They halted finally and drew back.

Fargo shifted position as he watched the chief face the squaws and touch one of the younger ones on the shoulder. Bare-breasted, with nice, rounded breasts, she stepped forward and one of the men handed her two flat stones. Approaching Hobbs with a swaying walk, she dropped to her knees in front of him and Fargo saw Hobbs' eyes were wide with terror. With a quick motion, she slammed the two flat stones together against Hobbs' testicles; his scream of pain rose into the night, hung in the air as his broken cries followed it. Fargo felt himself wince as the squaw stepped back and walked from the captive.

Hobbs was cursing and sobbing in pain, unable to collapse only because he was bound hand and foot to the stake. Three braves stepped forward next. They paused beside the nearest fire and, using a stone scoop, picked up a handful of burning embers and each poured his scoopful over Hobbs' head. The shock of reddish hair caught fire in spots, flared up, and set the rest of the hair ablaze. "Oh, God, oh, Jeeezzz . . . iiiiieeeee," Hobbs screamed in agony as his reddened body twisted. His screams continued, the pure agony of excruciating pain, until one of the Assiniboin poured a hide-lined basket of water over his head.

Fargo's nostrils drew in the acrid odor of burned hair as Hobbs hung in the bonds, sobbing moans of pain coming from him. Only a few, still-smoking patches of his hair remained, the rest of his head a combination of blackened and burned red skin. Fargo tried to find pity for the man; he thought about the wagons filled with massacred men, women, and children and cast aside the emotion. But he did feel concern. He wanted Hobbs with enough strength left to get away and to talk.

As he watched, two squaws went to Hobbs and gave him water, which he gulped down with eager gratitude. No compassion, Fargo knew. The Assiniboin had another whole day of torture planned for Hobbs, pain that would make what he'd suffered this night seem mild by comparison. They wanted him alive and aware. Sometimes they fed and treated captives in between torture to keep their strength up. He doubted they'd do that with Hobbs, and he saw two braves walk to the man and untie his bonds. Hobbs instantly sank to the ground, where he lay groaning. A brave seized him by one arm while the other did the same. They turned him on his back, his arms pulled straight out as two other braves stepped up with lances. They plunged the lances into his forearms and pinned him to the ground as he screamed in pain.

Laughing, they left him there and returned to the chief to sit down beside the fire and eat. Hobbs lay moaning, pinned to the ground.

The Assiniboin ate, the squaws stopped their wailing, and Hobbs was left pinned to the ground until the moon was high in the sky. They went to him then, pulled the lances from his arms, and retied him to the stake, where he sagged against the rawhide bonds. Fargo watched as the chief stepped into his tepee and the others went into theirs. Some of the squaws settled down on blankets outside the tepee and a few of the braves did the same.

But the camp was hardly more than a third of what it once was, and those left were exhausted with anger and fatigue. They slept quickly and Fargo waited until the camp was still before he crept forward. Flattening himself when he reached the edge of the camp, he began to crawl toward the figure tied to the stake. He stayed on his stomach, inching his way forward as he had once before in the Indian camp. He didn't rise till he reached Hobbs. He put a hand on the man's shoulder and Hobbs flinched and managed to pull his eyes open. "Don't talk," Fargo whispered even as he realized it was perhaps a needless command. He pulled the throwing knife from the calf holster around his leg and severed the rawhide bonds.

They had left Hobbs' clothes in a pile nearby and Fargo scooped up shirt and trousers, saw that the man's skin was too tender to put them on, and shoved them into his own belt. He glanced around him at the camp. Nothing moved, and he risked the time to push Hobbs' boots on him, his feet the only part of his body not raw from beating, scalding, or direct fire. He pulled the man up from where he had collapsed to the ground and Hobbs groaned and promptly collapsed again. Fargo dropped, spun, his eyes sweeping the camp, the Colt in his hand. But nothing moved. He drew a deep breath, reached down, and lifted Hobbs' naked body over his shoulder. Walking upright, he backed from the sleeping camp, his gaze flickering from one end to the other, the Colt still in his hand. He murmured a silent prayer of thanks as his luck held out and he reached the trees, turned, and made his way to where he'd left the Ovaro.

Hobbs was a big man and grew heavy quickly. His low moans were of more concern and Fargo was relieved when he spotted the horse. He lay Hobbs on his stomach across the saddle and the man groaned in pain. Swinging onto the horse behind Hobbs, Fargo sent the Ovaro through the trees as the first light of the new day began to touch the sky. He put the horse into a trot and ignored Hobbs' groans of pain. An hour passed and the dawn came in with the new sun. The Trailsman halted the horse to bend over Hobbs. "Talk," he said. "Where is she? Why twenty-four hours? What'd you do with her?"

But Hobbs looked at him with glazed, uncomprehending eyes and Fargo swore as he put the horse into a canter. He rode toward the cabin, scanned the terrain for familiar markings, and drew upon his memory.

The morning wore on, the cold staying in the air, not that it mattered any to Hobbs' battered body. But Fargo counted off the hours. There were only a half-dozen left before the twenty-four-hour period would be reached. He half-lifted Hobbs' body and saw only the blank stare. He sent the Ovaro into a gallop, holding Hobbs on the horse with one hand.

"What did you mean, goddamn you?" Fargo shouted as he rode. "What did you mean?" But the bouncing, jouncing naked form emitted only moaning sounds, garbled grunting noises that meant nothing even to himself.

Fargo kept the pinto at a full gallop, skirting trees, finally emerging from the heavy woodland to race across clear terrain. He recognized marks now, the man's cabin not more than another hour away. But the sun was beginning to drop over the low hills. Not more than another two hours to go before the time was past, perhaps irrevocably past. He glanced down at Hobbs. The man jounced in silence now, and Fargo forced himself to slow the pinto's gallop. Hobbs could give out at any moment, he realized. He'd no idea how much stamina the man possessed.

But he had no choice. He had to go on. He could only hope that Hobbs had her in his cabin, tied and facing a shotgun he had somehow rigged to go off within twenty-four hours. The sound of white water came to him soon and he glimpsed the raging rapids to his left. The cabin was close and he forced himself not to let the Ovaro go full out. Hobbs hadn't moaned in too long a time. The shallow hill came up and Fargo sent the Ovaro up it, the cabin coming into sight through the trees. He reined to a halt in front of the half-open door and his feet hit the ground before the Ovaro came to a full stop.

"Robin," he shouted as he raced into the cabin and came to a halt. The single room was empty. It stared mockingly back at him and he flung an oath into the silence.

8

Fargo whirled and ran from the cabin. He yanked Hobbs from the horse and dragged him into the cabin by one arm. The man breathed, uttering small moans as Fargo dropped him in the center of the floor. Though Hobbs had lain naked across the saddle in the very chilly air for most of the day, his body was still hot to the touch, burning from outside and in.

Fargo ran out to where he had noted the small well, drew up a bucket of the icy water, and ran into the cabin. He flung it over Hobbs, saw the man's body react, a flinching movement. He ran out and returned with another bucket.

This time Hobbs drew his knees up after he flinched as the icy water slammed over him. He was coming around, Fargo saw as he ran for another bucket of water. But the sun had disappeared behind the hills, he saw, and he was shouting curses as he flung another bucket of water over Hobbs. The man's eyes came open and he stared as if sightless.

"Where is she, damn you?" Fargo shouted as he saw Hobbs trying to focus on him. "What'd you do with her?" He saw Hobbs become conscious, his eyes blinking. A groan of pain escaped the man's lips and he reached for his crotch as he fell onto his side, started to draw his knees up in a fetal position.

Fargo yanked him onto his back and Hobbs screamed in pain, his eyes wide with terror as he saw Fargo's fist drawn back. "No, no more. Can't take any more pain," Hobbs gasped out. "Oh, Jesus, no."

"Where is she, goddamn you?" Fargo shouted, and his fist trembled as he fought to stop from smashing it into the man's face.

Hobbs stared in terror at him. "White water," he gasped. "Half-mile down."

Fargo spun and was racing full speed as he reached the Ovaro. He vaulted into the saddle and the horse spun, picking up unspoken commands. Fargo raced down the slope, through the stand of oak to the edge of the raging rapids, where he turned downstream and sent the horse along the very edge of the water. A mound of high rocks made him turn away from the shore and race around them, and he saw the dusk filtering down as he returned to the edge of the water. Peering ahead, he suddenly spied the object in the middle of the churning rapids.

It took shape, became a canoe, and he saw the length of lariat that reached from around the thin trunk of a sapling black oak to the canoe. Pulled by the force of the raging water, the canoe was held in midstream. Fargo glimpsed the flurry of flaxen hair as Robin raised her head. She saw him skid to a halt and he could barely hear her voice over the roaring hiss of the rushing water. "I'm tied," she shouted. "My wrists and ankles."

Fargo's eyes went to the end of the rope around the thin tree trunk. For twenty-four hours, maybe more, the raging waters had pulled at the canoe to sweep it downstream. For twenty-four hours that single strand of rope had been pulled so taut that it had begun to fray where it circled the tree trunk. Hobbs had calculated almost perfectly, Fargo cursed silently. The rope was frayed almost to the last strands. He moved the horse closer, and as he did, one of the last strands gave way. The remaining, frayed strands would break if he touched them. If he left them alone, they might hold another two or three minutes.

And he heard another sound, the deep roar of the waterfall, not more than another half-mile away. He peered across the churning water into the canoe as he considered using his own lariat. But he discarded the thought. Robin was too deep inside the canoe, and even if he did drop the rope over her, she couldn't slip it around herself. The snap of another strand parting brought his eyes to the rope. Two minutes left, he grimaced. Trying to pull the canoe in would never work. Even if he managed to hang on to the rope as it gave way, and avoided being pulled into the stream himself, the canoe would spin and turn over and it'd be Robin's finish, tied as she was.

The canoe would float freely when the rope gave way, light enough to be swept downstream on the crest of the racing water. There was one chance of saving her, and that meant he had to be in midrapids when the rope shredded. He brought a hard slap down on the Ovaro's rump and the horse shot into an instant gallop along the edge of the rushing water. A hundred yards on he spied the tree branch leaning out over the shore; he reined to a halt and yanked his lariat from the saddle as he leapt to the ground. He flung one end over the branch, tightened it securely, and wrapped a dozen turns of the rope around his waist. He'd used up another minute and he kicked off boots, shed gun belt, and plunged into the racing water. He was swept out and downstream at once and he swam toward the middle of the racing, frothing water as he was swept downward.

He could see the column of misty spray that marked the falls rising into the air some hundred yards away. He kept fighting to go sideways as the water swept him along. Somehow, he managed to reach the center of the rapids as a crest of foam swept over him. He went down, came up spitting water, and saw that he was a few yards past midstream but still being swept downstream when suddenly he was yanked to a halt. The sharp stop jarred him from head to toe as the lariat came to an end, only one knotted loop still around his waist.

But he was no longer being swept downstream. He gulped in deep breaths between rushing crests of foam that swept over him. The raging water angrily pulled at him, demanding its victim, and as he surfaced once again, he saw the canoe rushing toward him, precariously rising on the crests of the frothing, hurtling waters. It would pass a dozen yards to his left, he saw, and he began to pull himself forward on the rope until he was almost directly in front of it. The canoe rose up only a few feet from him, hung on a foaming crest, and then came down hard. He released his hold on the rope and grabbed at the side of the canoe with both hands. It went over at once, Robin falling out and almost on top of him.

She started to go down, but he got one arm around her neck and pulled her head out of the water. Her eyes, wide with terror, stared at him in disbelief. But the water had pulled him downstream again and only the rope prevented him from being swept away. He felt the jar go through his body again as he was yanked to a halt. Keeping his left arm around Robin's neck, holding her head barely out of the water against his shoulder, he began to pull himself along the lariat with his right hand. He had gone not more than a few dozen feet when it seemed as though he'd gone a mile. The muscles of his arm burned and he could feel the knots in his shoulder. Another dozen feet and he felt the strength all but gone from his right arm. But a stone rose from the water a few feet above where he'd stopped and it sent the racing waters leaping to both sides and crested a small, oblong pocket of relatively calm water.

He used the watery island of calm to shift Robin to his other side and she helped by kicking her bound legs outward. Wrapping his strained right arm around her neck, he began to pull them forward again with his left arm. The shore was growing closer, yet it seemed a thousand yards away as he felt the pain start to shoot through his left arm. He paused, held himself still as the water leapt over him, and he shot a glance at Robin. She was all right, her face tight with fear, but her eyes clear as she returned his glance. He began to pull again and halted after each second pull to rest his arm muscles.

Dusk had descended and the day was quickly sliding into night. He pulled again, his lips drawn back in pain as he kept pulling, and he felt the strength ebbing from his body.

But the shore was close now, beckoning, encouraging the will and the flesh. He was cursing with the pain as he pulled, and it seemed as though his arm was about to pull from his shoulder socket. But suddenly the force of the water lessened and the shore was but a few more feet away. Two last, pain-racked pulls on the rope and he felt the bank under his feet. He pushed himself forward, a knee sinking into soft ground now; another push and he lay face-down on the soft dark-green mat of nut moss. His arm fell away from Robin and she lay alongside him, listening to the harsh, rasping sound of his breath as he drew in deep drafts of air.

He lay unmoving until the quivering ceased in his arms and the night came to spread its black blanket before he pushed his palms into the moss and sat up. He drew the knife from its calf holster and cut the ropes binding Robin's wrists and ankles. She came against him, arms around his neck, clinging to him until he pushed her back.

"Get up, get out of those wet clothes," he said as he felt himself shiver in the cold of the night air. "I'll get you a blanket," he said, and went to his saddlebag.

He pulled an extra blanket out, tossed it to her, and she stepped behind the trees. Not that she needed to. He could hardly see her in the blackness. He pulled off clothes as he groped along the ground and found enough twigs to get a fire started. When the small spurt of flame rose, he was all but naked and had enough light to find larger pieces of wood to feed the fire. The flames spiraled higher, sent out more warmth, but even so he shivered in the cold of the night. He took down his bedroll. Robin appeared, wrapped in the blanket, and she spread her clothes out in front of the fire as he had his, somehow managing to be efficient and modest at the same time.

Half inside the warmth of his bedroll, he lay back and felt the pain in his arms still there.

Robin folded herself beside him inside the blanket. "Tell me," she said, and he proceeded to recount everything that had happened. She was staring at him with guilt in her eyes when he finished.

"My fault," she murmured. "All because of that one night."

"Part of it," he agreed. "You nearly got yourself killed because you had to satisfy your damn curiosity."

"Yes," she said gravely. "But not just curiosity. Anger, hurt, frustration, and maybe something else. It all came together. Everything except self-discipline."

"What was the something else?" he asked.

"It doesn't matter now," she said. "But I think you

should leave me here. Forget about me. I'm bad news."

"I'll go along with that," he said, and waited to catch a quick glare. But there was none. Only a nod as she looked down at the blanket around her. "But I'll take you back to Lakeside. I don't like leaving things half-done." She said nothing and he lay back and she saw him wince.

"Your arms still hurting?" she asked.

"Arms, shoulders, back."

"Turn on your stomach," she said, and pulled the blanket around her as she freed her arms. He flipped onto his stomach and felt her hands on his back, rubbing, massaging, first along his back, then his shoulders, and then each arm. It felt wonderful. She had a good touch, strong enough and smooth, and he felt his muscles respond to her gentle kneading. He also felt the edge of the blanket touching his back as it dropped from around her while she moved her arms. He wanted to turn his head to glance back, but she finished and pulled the blanket in place again at once.

"Better?" she asked.

"Much better," he said. "Where'd you learn that?"

"My mother was subject to back spasms," she answered, and sank back on the blanket beside him.

"What'd he do with your wagon and horses?" Fargo asked.

"Hid them in the woods behind the cabin."

"He do anything to you?"

"No. He was saving that for when he came back, he told me," she said. "He expected to be back in plenty of time to pull the canoe in."

"The best-laid plans . . ." Fargo muttered. "Get some sleep. It'll take another hour or so for the clothes to dry out."

"Yes," she said. "I'm drained."

His body echoed her words and he closed his

eyes and sleep was upon him at once. He woke a little over an hour later and saw that Robin was deep in slumber and felt the exhaustion still in his arms and shoulders. They'd stay the night, he decided. Hobbs would be in the cabin, come morning. He was in no condition to go anywhere. Fargo turned on his side and embraced sleep for the rest of the night, not at all unhappy to do so.

The new day dawned in its own time, cold and crisp, and he sat up. The fire had gone out, but the clothes were dry. He rose and dressed as Robin woke. She shook the tangle of flaxen hair and it sprayed sunlight in all directions. She rose, the blanket kept around her, gathered her clothes, and went behind a tree. She emerged looking rested, but her face was still tight, the recent days still with her. They'd stay, he grunted silently, longer than she wanted. He climbed up on the Ovaro, reached a hand down, pulled her onto the saddle in front of him, and felt the warm softness of her rear against him.

"What about Hobbs or whatever his name?" Robin asked as they rode.

"I'll take him back," Fargo said. "You'll have trouble recognizing him."

"I'll recognize him. I'll never forget him," Robin said grimly, and settled into silence as they neared the cabin.

Fargo saw the cabin door open, but he had flung it open as he raced away. But caution was as much a part of him as it was the mountain lion and he drew the Colt as he halted and let Robin slide from the saddle.

"Stay here," he muttered as he dismounted and crossed to the cabin door in three quick steps, pausing against the wall for a moment, then bursting into the cabin in a crouch, the Colt raised and ready to fire. But the large room was empty. Hobbs had gone.

Fargo felt the disbelief swirl through him. He knelt down on the floor of rough boards and traced the bloodstains. A smear of red led to one wall where the clothes pegs were empty, then trailed to the cabin door. Hobbs had taken some clothes and somehow, someway, had found the strength to pull himself from the cabin.

Fargo grimaced. He should have known. He had seen terribly wounded animals do unbelievable things, drawing on the greatest strength of all: the will to survive. He had underestimated Hobbs' will and his physical stamina.

Fargo turned and stepped from the cabin to freeze, the curse catching in his throat. Seven bare-chested Assiniboin faced him with drawn bows, an eighth one holding Robin. The round-chested chief waited to one side, his black eyes glittering bits of coal. Fargo whispered curses. They had been lying in wait in the trees and had seen him arrive with Robin. They had followed his tracks when they woke and found Hobbs gone. Or they possibly knew the location of the cabin and went there assuming it was where Hobbs had gone.

It didn't much matter. They had come, waited, and now he was in their hands. The chief stepped forward, lifted the Colt from its holster, and threw the gun to one of the braves. Fargo knew enough Siouan to converse and more than enough sign language to help him along.

"You are the one who set him free," the Indian said, and Fargo nodded. The Indian's black-coal eyes narrowed further. Fargo's thoughts raced. Boldness was the only way that might help him. He had tricked the Indian into losing three-quarters of his warriors, a tactical defeat. Now he had to trick him into a personal defeat. It was the only chance for Robin and him to stay alive.

"He did not betray you. I did," Fargo said, and

saw surprise flood the Indian's broad face. "I tricked him and I tricked you."

Fury replaced surprise in the Indian's face, but he was canny, suspicious of Fargo's admission. "Why did you free him?" he questioned. Fargo gave him the answer he would understand and accept.

"He was mine to kill," Fargo said, and the Indian's silence signified his acceptance. "And now you are mine to kill," Fargo said. "Hobbs was a jackal. The Assiniboin are vultures."

"You are mad and stupid," the Indian chief snapped. "My warriors will answer you."

"Let the chief answer me himself," Fargo said as he smiled. "He kills me or I kill him." Fargo used sign language to emphasize the challenge. Man to man, he indicated, and his eyes flicked to the others and saw them waiting for the chief to answer. "The great chief has weapons," Fargo said. "A skinning knife and a tomahawk in his waistband. I have no weapons. Is the great chief afraid to fight someone without weapons?"

The fury strained the Indian's face. He had been pushed into a corner, his warriors waiting. For him to refuse would be to lose face, perhaps to lose command. Fargo read the thoughts as they raced through the man's mind. He had put them there with the challenge. But he knew something more now: the Assiniboin chief feared man-to-man combat. He was unsure of himself, a man no longer filled with confidence in his own abilities. The fear came in many ways, age sometimes, the knowledge that he could no longer move with his former quickness.

But the chief was trapped. He could not turn aside the challenge. The Indian's weaknesses could work for him and against him, Fargo realized. The man would be doubly dangerous because he'd need to go all out. He had the weapons, but he'd be prone to make mistakes. The advantages were a toss-up.

Fargo stepped back as the Assiniboin motioned to his men and they lowered their bows. The act was a reply and the Indian chief took out the tomahawk first, gripped it in his right hand while he held the skinning knife in his left.

He began to circle and Fargo circled with him, his eyes flicking to the Indian's moccasined feet. The man moved heavily. Fargo smiled inwardly, but the smile vanished as he had to leap away from a swinging blow of the tomahawk followed by a slash of the knife that narrowly missed his shoulder. The man's hand speed was fast, and he came in low, crouching, feinted a blow, and the chief's tomahawk came crashing down only inches from his wrist. Fargo weaved again, danced, feinted, and drew a double slash of tomahawk and knife. Both missed and the man was off-balance, unable to spin as Fargo came in with a pile-driver blow into the Indian's kidney.

The Assiniboin stumbled forward with a grunt of pain, but he whirled fast enough to prevent Fargo from landing another blow. Fargo weaved again, feinted a looping left, and the Assiniboin countered with a cross-over slash of the knife that caught Fargo by surprise. The Trailsman twisted away and saw the tomahawk crash down. He felt it scrape along the side of his temple and a sharp pain shot through his head. He flung himself sideways, hit the ground on his back, and saw the Assiniboin diving at him with tomahawk and skinning knife upraised.

Fargo's kicked upward with both legs, both boots catching the Indian squarely in the groin as he dived. The red man's mouth fell open in pain as he shuddered in midair and toppled to one side. Fargo leapt as he spun, sent a sharp left crashing down against the Assiniboin's cheekbone, and the man fell back on one knee. The chief tried to turn again, but Fargo's sledgehammer blow smashed down on the back of his neck. The Assiniboin went down and Fargo brought his foot down on the hand with the tomahawk. He heard the Indian's cry of pain as his knuckles were crushed. Fargo scooped up the short-handled ax.

He stepped a half-pace back to bring it down and saw the Indian, half on his back, send the skinning knife hurtling through the air with a short, flipping motion. It was no throwing blade, but Fargo felt its serrated edge cut through his shirt and into his chest. He staggered back a step as he brushed the knife loose with his left arm and glanced up to see the Indian charging him, both hands outstretched to close around his throat. He tried to step back again, but the man's bull-like charge carried him forward. Fargo felt the big hands encircle his throat. Battling with desperation fueled by fear, the Indian held him in a viselike grip, his weight pinning Fargo on his back. Fargo felt his breath being shut off almost instantaneously. Freeing his arm, he brought the tomahawk up in a flat arc and crashed the side of the ax against the Indian's head.

The man's grip loosened as he half-fell to the side, enough for Fargo to bring his other fist up and sink it into the Indian's stomach with a short, upward blow. The Assiniboin toppled onto his side. Fargo brought the tomahawk around in a short arc.

It smashed into the Indian's forehead and he fell backward as a line of red erupted across his brow. It was a hard blow, but not fatal, and Fargo stepped back. He let the man stagger to his feet. He gave him the chance to accept defeat even as he knew the Assiniboin would never take it. The man swayed, braced himself, and emitted a screaming roar of anguish and fury as he charged forward again. Fargo dropped the tomahawk and brought up a whistling left that smashed into the Indian's jaw. The man halted, gasped, and Fargo's right crashed into his jaw again. The Indian chief went down, quivered, and slowly turned and pushed up onto his hand and knees. Fargo suddenly saw the skinning knife on the grass only inches from the man's hand.

The Assiniboin saw it, too, seized it, and pushed to his feet with a last surge of victory in his grasp. He charged, lashing out with the knife in a wide swinging arc. Fargo held his ground to the last moment, and as the serrated edge of the blade whistled at his throat, he dropped low, to one knee. He felt the blade swoosh through his hair and the Indian bumped against him. Fargo brought his hand up, his fingers closing around the man's wrist. Using the rest of his body as leverage, he spun his foe in a half-circle, released his grip on the man's wrist, and smashed his forearm against the Indian's hand, all the driving power of his body behind it. The skinning knife plunged sideways into the Assiniboin chief's throat and the man staggered back, his mouth falling open to utter short, rasping sounds as the blood poured down his chest.

He sank to his knees, stayed there for a moment, and then pitched forward onto his face. He gave a last shudder and lay still.

Fargo stepped back, turned, and swept the line of warriors with narrowed eyes. Two stepped forward to where their chief lay and began to drag the lifeless form away. The one holding Robin took his hands from her and another dropped the Colt on the ground. Carrying their chief with them, they faded back into the trees and Fargo heard the sound of their ponies moving away.

Robin rushed to Fargo and it was only then that he was conscious of the warm, sticky red that ran down his own chest. She took him into the cabin as he opened his shirt and sat down atop the pile of pelts.

"Stay here. I've some rags in my wagon," she

said, and ran outside. He heard the creak of the wagon returning a few minutes later and she appeared with the rags, some wet with water from the well, and quickly cleaned the wound. It was not deep, but it took a while to stanch the flow of blood. But she finally had it bandaged with long strips that she tied behind his back.

He rested awhile and then rose. "Time to start back," he said, and she nodded and followed him outside. She drove the wagon and he rode beside her, a slow, unhurried pace. They were halfway to Lakeside when she asked the question. It had been swirling through his mind, but he had no good answer.

"What about Hobbs?" she said.

"Nothing," he said. "Maybe he managed to get away, find a place to hide. And maybe he collapsed and bought it before he got very far. He was in bad shape, real bad shape."

"We just write him off," she said.

"Unless I come onto something that tells me differently. There's been enough fighting and killing for now," Fargo said, and she nodded agreement.

They reached Lakeside as his eyes swept the sky. It had turned slate, a snow sky, and the wind had a new bite to it. The day was nearing an end and he rode to the inn with her before he went on to see the sheriff.

Tom Draper listened to the story and sat back with a sigh of wonderment when Fargo finished.

"It came apart, but you managed to put it back together, the important pieces, at least," the sheriff said. "You're a special man, Fargo. I heard as much. Now I can say I know it for myself. What about the girl?"

"I'm riding south. I'll take her with me," Fargo said. "I was looking at the sky. There's an early snow coming in a day or two, I'd guess."

"Old man winter likes to give us a real preview sometimes," Tom said. "I'll have my boys keep an eye out for Hobbs. If he's still alive and anywhere near here, we'll spot him."

"Good enough," Fargo said, and left with a warm handshake. He had decided not to visit Vera. Their time together had been perfect and he was going to leave, come morning. It was best left the way it was. But when he reached the inn, he found Robin outside, a short jacket on against the cold, her eyes peering north in the last light of the day. She turned when he came up, and he saw her wipe the tears from one eye. She set her face tight.

"The time's gone now," he said. "It was never there for you."

She didn't answer and he saw the determination in the set of her jaw as she continued to peer northward. "It's not really that far from here," she said.

"Damn, you're still thinking about going, aren't you?"

"If you helped me," she said. "I'm sure I could make it. Something good should come out of all that's happened."

"And that'd be you holed up doing your wildlife research," he said, and she nodded.

"I'm going south tomorrow. I figured to see you get back safe," he said.

"I'll likely go along with you, but I'll always know I could've made it," she said.

He stared at her for a long moment and then turned away. At the inn he got the same room he'd had before, and left her staring northward. He stretched out on the bed and her last words stayed with him. She'd spend the entire winter thinking she could have made it, berating herself for not just plunging on alone. She'd convince herself more and more with each passing day until inner certainty became an uncontested fact. And she'd be miserable all winter as she clutched that conviction to her.

He undressed, closed his eyes, and his thoughts were still on Robin. She was so goddamn sure she could make it she deserved to be convinced, he muttered inwardly, and a small smile edged his lips as he fell asleep.

9

Fargo rose early and the sky was still slate. He had biscuits and coffee at the inn and then went to visit Tom Draper. When he left, he was armed with what he wanted to know. He returned to the inn to find Robin checking the gear on the wagon. In between glances northward, he noted.

"You coming with me?" he asked, and she offered a half-shrug.

"Doesn't appear I've a lot of choice," she said.

"You can go on by yourself."

"Don't tempt me," she flared.

"You going to spend the whole damn winter thinking you could've done it?"

"Probably," she admitted.

"All right, you want to go so damn badly, I'll take you," he said, and watched her mouth fall open in astonishment.

"You mean that?"

"I mean it. And it means we move right now. Every damn minute will count," he said.

She flung her arms around him, the flaxen hair in his face, and then she pulled back, suspicion in her eyes as she peered at him. "Why?" she asked. "Why the sudden change of heart? You've been saying it couldn't be done and now you say I can do it."

He had expected the question. She was sharp and full of thorniness. "I had a talk with Tom Draper.

He told me a route that'll cut enough time to make it," Fargo said blandly, and she thought over the answer for only a few seconds. Eagerness and excitement allowed no more than that.

"I'll get the things from my room and be right out." She started to rush away, then turned, pressed her lips on his with a quick kiss of happy enthusiasm and gratitude, the kind bestowed by little girls at birthday parties. He waited for her to return with the same small smile that had edged his lips when he had fallen asleep during the night.

Robin came back quickly and Fargo led the way north out of town. He immediately set a northeast course that skirted the Mesabi Range and he held a fast pace. The wind was colder, the sky grayer when he called a halt an hour before dark in a place surrounded by dried, fallen trees.

"You said you brought axes," he told Robin. "Get them out and let's cut enough firewood to load into the back of the wagon."

"Can't we cut firewood as we go along?" she asked.

"We mightn't find a spot like this," he said.

She shrugged and brought out two axes and worked beside him splitting the dry wood until darkness fell. He made a small cooking fire, warmed the beef strips, and she ate in tired silence beside him. When he set out his bedroll, she put her blanket alongside and he was almost asleep when he heard her voice, soft in the darkness.

"Thank you, Fargo," she half-whispered. "For everything . . . and especially for this."

"Go to sleep," he said, and she obeyed at once.

In the morning, the slate sky had lowered and the wind swept across the open plateaus. He turned more eastward and found a line of bigtooth aspen that helped break up the wind. Robin drove with a scarf around her face that stopped just below her eyes.

He increased the pace across a stretch of flat terrain and by midday the snow began. No slow, gentle start but a flurry of wind-driven flakes, followed by others that came down at an angle in the strong wind. Fargo cursed silently. He wasn't where he wanted to be, and he kept the pace despite the snow, which now swept at them with white fury.

The ground was well-covered by midafternoon and he squinted as he peered through the driving snowstorm. The temperature had dropped and he slowed to let Robin catch up to him.

She pulled the scarf from around her mouth and shouted at him. "We've got to find someplace to hole up," she said.

"This is flat country for another fifty miles," he told her. "A heavy stand of aspen is the best I can do." He waved forward and rode on.

The snow made visibility a precarious thing and he felt his eyes smarting as he strained to see ahead. The line of bigtooth aspen had been one of the markers Tom Draper had mentioned, so Fargo knew he was in the right area. He'd gone perhaps another mile when he spotted the tall slab of granite that rose all by itself, a monument to nothing. He uttered a snort of satisfaction, made a sharp right turn a hundred feet past the stone, and rode on, pausing only to make sure Robin was following behind.

The storm had begun to howl, winds screaming down with fury, and there were six inches of snow on the ground when he saw the shape rise up to his right. He veered toward it, head bent low against a sharp flurry of wind-driven snow, and raised his eyes to see the house. He rode to a halt in front of it and waited for Robin to roll up. It was pretty much as Tom Draper had described: a neo-Gothic monstrosity now pretty much a wreck. There had been two corner towers and both had collapsed. The side of one wall of the center of the house had fallen in on itself, but he saw that the barn was in good shape and still attached to the rear of the house. He motioned to Robin as she reached him; he led the way into the barn, dismounted, and unsaddled the Ovaro while she drove the wagon to one side.

"My God, what luck," she breathed.

"No luck. Tom Draper told me about it," Fargo said. "It's called Eklund's Folly. The man built it out here in the middle of nowhere and found he couldn't stand the terrible winters. He left it and it's been falling apart ever since, a little more each winter, until one day it'll just be a pile of rubble. But the barn's still good, as Tom said, and there's a fireplace. Though the wind comes in from everywhere, we'll have a roof over our heads."

"I'm happy for anything," she said, and he stepped into what had been the main room of the house. A pair of mattresses were scattered on the floor. They were not the only ones who had made use of Eklund's Folly. He saw the large stone fireplace and walked to the wagon. "Unload the firewood, honey. We'll need every damn log of it," he said, and she helped as he carried the wood into the room and stacked it against one wall. He felt the walls of the house shake as a particularly hard gust of wind blew. He got the fire started before night descended.

Robin unhitched the team and fed them as Fargo brought the fire to a nice, steady flame that brought a circle of warmth to at least part of the cavernous room.

Robin brought some food from her wagon and found some pots and pans in the kitchen along with mounds of snow that came in through holes in the ceiling. They ate hot beans and dried bacon and had a johnnycake each as the storm howled outside. He saw the snow that came into the house along the line of the collapsed wall, but it was a room away. He finally took down his bedroll and spread it out as the fire burned down to warm embers.

"I'm going to get some sleep," he said, and began to undress.

Robin went to the wagon to change into her nightdress and returned shivering, her blanket in hand. He saw her eyes move across his muscled symmetry as he lay more out of the sleeping bag than in, and she finally lay down, turned her back to him, and he listened to her fall asleep.

He smiled. She had been touched by alarm and surprise at the ferocity of the storm. She'd felt the fear, and tomorrow she'd know the reality. He slept contentedly as the storm grew worse outside. When morning came, he found a bucket, melted snow in it to use to wash with, and didn't need to step outside. He had another bucket of snow melted and ready for Robin when she woke, and he went to the barn and fed the horses while she washed. When he returned to the living room, she was at the window, staring out at at least four feet of snow that didn't seem to be stopping.

"Why don't you go out and get some more firewood?" he asked, and she turned and stared at him. "Or maybe shoot some game?" he added.

"It's not amusing."

"Wasn't meant to be," he said cheerfully.

She turned away to stare out the window again until finally she went into the kitchen, found an iron kettle, and fetched a tin of tea from her wagon.

After they breakfasted, Fargo stirred the fire again, added another log, and stretched out on his bedroll. Robin restlessly went to the window every half-hour to stare out, and he saw her face grow tighter each time.

It was midday when he rose, stretched, and started to pull on a jacket and heavy coat he'd brought in from his saddlepack. "Get your clothes on," he said.

"We can't leave, not in this," Robin said, alarm instant in her voice.

"We're going out, you and me," he said.

"Why?" She frowned.

"Tell you later," he said, and the frown stayed with her as she donned a sweater, then another, and a full-length cape. He led the way out through the barn and the wind slammed into him as he stepped outside. He began to trudge away, the storm still blinding in its fury. Robin followed, close at his heels, but floundered through drifts that were at least six feet in height. He felt the storm's fury biting into him as he fought his way forward. Robin followed, with more difficulty now, he saw as she fell more often. They had left sight of the house, but she was unaware that he was making a long, wide circle, one he planned would take at least two hours to complete.

They had gone on for perhaps an hour more when he heard Robin's cry. He turned, to see her sprawled in the snow. He went back and pulled her to her feet.

"I can't go on," she gasped. "This is stupid. Let's go back."

"No," he snapped, and pulled her along with him.

She wrested her arm free after a few moments, to flounder alongside him, and when she went down again, he saw the pain in her face. He pulled her to her feet and held on to her this time as he made a sharp turn. They had almost completed the wide circle and he pushed toward the house, only fairly certain he moved in the right direction. He was off by a hundred yards and he glimpsed the house in the distant left as the snow lightened for a few minutes. He shifted course and the storm was back in all its fury as he reached the house and half-dragged Robin into the barn. She stumbled and he heard her harsh, labored breathing as he helped her to the living room and the fire.

She sank down, trembling, stayed almost prone in front of the fire for at least fifteen minutes before she rose and pulled off her outer clothes. When she'd taken off the second sweater, she turned and faced him, her breathing still hard and her breasts heaving under her shirt. "Why, dammit?" she asked. "Why'd you do that?"

"I was playing make-believe," he said. "But suppose it was for real. Suppose you were out alone in the north country in a storm twice this bad. Suppose you were out looking for game when the storm came up. They can do that out of nowhere. Or suppose your horse ran off and you went out looking for him." He rose, pulled her to her feet, and pushed her to the window, where the snow all but stopped her from seeing out. "I don't figure this'll last more than another day, but in the north country they can last for a week at a time. You see any game to shoot moving around out there? You see any firewood to gather out there?"

He took his hand from her arm and stalked back to the fireplace and sat down on the bedroll.

She came in a slow walk, her robin's-egg-blue eyes spearing him with a frown of appraisal. "That's why you did this, isn't it? That's why we're here. You never intended taking me all the way," she said.

"Go to the head of the class," he said. A vicious gust of wind shook the walls and he saw Robin flinch. "Just a sample, honey," he said.

"And an object lesson," she added, her eyes narrowed on him.

He shrugged. "Let's say it'll be damn hard for you to spend the winter telling yourself you could've made it," he replied.

She sat quietly, took her eyes from him, and stared into the fire. She stayed that way until the night came. He added another log to the fire.

"I'll make us dinner," she said quietly, and rose and moved away without a backward glance. She took more things from the wagon and fashioned a meal of tinned beef cooked in the iron skillet with corn and two baked potatoes.

"That was right good," Fargo said when they finished, and he helped carry the tin plates into the kitchen. He warmed a bucket of snow water and let the dishes soak in it. When he returned to the living room, Robin was at the window, staring at the snow, which still fell. He stretched out before the fire and she spoke from beside the window, a sadness in her voice.

"I've been such a fool, haven't I?" she said. "I wouldn't listen at all."

"Dreams can make fools of the best of us. I've seen it happen before."

She turned from the window and came to stand over him, looking down at him, her face thoughtful. "Remember when I said I waited outside Vera's because I was hurt and angry and frustrated? And I said there was something more?" she asked, and he nodded. "That something more was jealousy," she said, and drew a raised eyebrow from him. "I wouldn't admit it, not even to myself, but that's what it was. You'd saved my life twice over. I felt that meant you cared about me. Or maybe that's just what I wanted to feel. And I was jealous, plain and simple jealous."

"Confession's good for the soul, I've been told," Fargo said.

"Yes, but it doesn't do much for the body," she said, and she ran her hand down the front of her shirt and pulled the garment open. She flung it aside and he stared up at lovely, well-formed breasts, full-cupped and tapering to the top, each white mount tipped by a very pink nipple that lay flat against an equally pink circle. He saw nicely rounded shoulders and a tapering waist that grew more so as Robin tossed aside her skirt and bloomers to stand magnificently naked in front of him. He took in wide hips, a flat abdomen, a small but thick little triangle, and long legs that were beautifully shaped with long thighs and round knees, sweeping calves, and small ankles.

Robin, without clothes, seemed a bigger girl than she did dressed, but everything balanced beautifully. He sat up and began to shed clothes. She didn't move as she stared down at him, her lips parted as she watched him undress. "I've never done this before," she murmured. "Undressed before a man like this."

"I'm honored," he said as his eyes swept over her again.

"I feel like a hussy, suddenly brazen," she said.

"Prove it." He smiled, reached up, and pulled her down to him.

Robin gave a little scream as their bodies touched, skins tingling against each other, and he fell back, held her atop him, and felt her breasts warm against him. He was rising, responding, and pushed up against her crotch.

"Oh, oh, my. Oh, my God," Robin gasped out, and her mouth fell on his, wildness in her kisses, her tongue darting out, pulling back, finding new purposes for itself. He rolled her onto her back and his mouth found one flat pink nipple, circled it with his tongue, and felt it rise and grow firm. Robin was crying out sounds, little burst of high-pitched squeals, utter pleasure in each, and he drew more of her breast into his mouth. She half-screamed and her head fell from side to side and the flaxen hair was a yellow shower.

Her lovely breasts shook as his hands moved down her body, came to the black little triangle, and his fingers pressed into the wiry nape to find a high little pubic mound. He sucked on one breast as he stroked her inner thighs. "Oh, oh . . . ooooooh, please, oh, yes, oh, careful . . . careful. Oh, my God," Robin cried out, jumbled words and jumbled emotions all mingling together in a special wild wanting. She snapped her head from side to side again as his hand moved up her thigh, came to the inner place where it met the wiry filaments of the dark little nap and found her skin moist. He slid his hand further, fingers touching warm wetness, lips of sequestered ecstasy, and Robin's little gasped cries became stronger.

"No, oh, no, no, no," she said as her hips rose against him and she pressed her pudenda into his palm. "No, no, no," she said again, and her hand found his and pushed him in deeper. The storm outside was matched by the storm inside, Fargo realized as he was swept away by her wildness. Her thighs had hardly parted when he slid over her, his own warmth moving along the wiry black nap, down to the dark portal.

Robin screamed as her legs opened, lifted, and he sank into her. "Jesus, oh, God . . . aaaaah, ah, ah," she flung out, sound made words, words made sounds, and he stayed with her, slowly at first. The sharp screams grew sharper, but there was pure ecstasy in each now, matching his every slow thrust until he felt her lovely body responding. She rose with him, fell back, rose, slow pumpings that grew faster, and he stayed with her, let her set the pace, and she pulled his face into her breasts as she screamed out with pleasure.

She surprised him another way. Her wildness held back against the final moment as she clasped her thighs around him and pulled and pumped and clasped his face first to one lovely cup and then the other. Screams were now blended into one endless paean of delight and still she somehow managed to hold back. Not with planning, he was sure, not even the wisdom of the senses but with an inner mechanism that protected ecstasy. But the senses were not to be denied their moment, and as she writhed and pumped with him, he suddenly felt her grow rigid. Her cries spiraled, became screams, wild, shrieking screams as the flaxen hair bounced up and down and sprayed out in all directions. Her lovely, full-cupped breasts quivered against his face, and her thighs were pressed tight to his waist. He felt the sweet squeezings of her around him, inner and outer squeezings, culminations rising as one, the world capsuled into a single moment.

The moment spiraled down all too quickly and Fargo heard her murmur of dismay and then she was lying against him, trembling in short bursts and then lying still again. Finally she pulled herself up alongside him to rest one lovely breast against his face as she settled down with him. He heard the sound of her steady breathing as she fell asleep, one pink tip resting against his lips, and he let her stay that way as he slept with her. During the night, she stirred, turned on her side, and he slipped away to add another log to the fire. He paused at the window to look at the snow that swirled outside, and quickly growing chilled, he hurried back to Robin and the warmth of the fire.

Morning came but no one dressed until Robin wrapped a shawl around herself to make tea. The old, battered, windswept house was almost as cold as the outside, except for the circle of warmth around the fire.

• Fargo drew on clothes later and saw to the horses. The barn was considerably warmer than the house, he found, its walls still tight and sturdy, and when he returned to the house, Robin was waiting for him in beautiful nakedness in front of the fire. She was as a child who had found a new toy and could not do without it.

The days and the nights melded together to become one long hymn to the senses. Robin was a total joy, reveling in every discovery she made about herself and about him.

When the storm ended, she offered a wry smile. "I prayed for the snow to stay away, and now I'm sorry it's stopped," she said.

"We still have the trip south," Fargo said, and she brightened at once. He helped her hitch the horses, saddled the Ovaro, and led the way from the barn. The snow was not too deep and they made fair time in the cold and crisp day. The storm hadn't extended far south, and by the following day they were in terrain free of snow but the air stayed crisp and clear. The nights were spend in his bedroll beside a small fire and he could almost forget the rest of the world.

The morning was cold as he rode beside the wagon, the late fall foliage still brilliant, the blazing stars giving their own color to the landscape with long beds of their pink-lavender ragged heads. "I'm going to come back next year," Robin said as they rode. "I'll come back early and give myself plenty of time. There's a woman, a few years older than I am, who was willing to come with me. She was a student of Professor Welby, too. Maybe I'll bring her along next time."

"That'd be good," Fargo said. "It's not a place for being alone. Too much can go wrong."

"I'll still need a trailsman," Robin said.

"Maybe," he allowed, and gave her the address where mail reached him.

For the most part, the days passed in simply enjoying the land and the nights in enjoying each other. It was the third day and they moved through low hill country with thick stands of black oak and mountain ash; he slowed the pace and enjoyed the swooping flights of slate-colored juncos, goldfinches, and the ever-present shiny black crows. He heard their constant chatter and the whooping calls of the juncos as he watched the deer move with casual calm, thick herds of white tails, their red-fawn coats already turning to winter gray.

Rugged grouse were extremely plentiful and every few hundred yards a covey sprang into the air on a whir of wings in their almost vertical flight. They were fun to watch as they kept exploding in a shower of feathers.

Fargo had moved Robin to the right, where a flat passage opened near a thick stand of low-branched hawthorns. They had gone another thousand yards or so when his eyes narrowed as they swept the land. Suddenly there were no explosions of grouse, no swooping flights of goldfinch and junco, and no deer moving casually nearby. Suddenly there was only silence, and Fargo felt the hairs stiffen on the back of his neck. Sudden silence meant one thing only: danger. The wild creatures sensed it, felt it, drew in the scent of danger each in their own ways. But they knew the feel of it, even when it wasn't directed at them, and they grew silent in caution and fear.

Fargo felt the explosion inside himself as he spun in the saddle, reached over, and yanked on the reins of the team. "Jump," he shouted to Robin.

"Get off the wagon. On the other side." He heard her gasp of surprise but glimpsed her turn and start to jump as he pulled the team to a halt. The shot exploded the silence and he saw the bullet hit the edge of the wagon seat as Robin disappeared over the other side.

Fargo dived from the saddle as the second shot rang out, and he heard the bullet whistle only inches from his head.

He hit the ground, rolled, flung himself sideways as another shot sent a shower of dirt but an inch from his leg. He managed to come up before the right front wheel of the wagon. To his left he saw Robin, flat on her stomach against the rear wheel. Another shot tore splinters from the wheel spokes. Rifle fire, Fargo swore, too powerful and too accurate to be anything else. From inside the hawthorns and he and Robin were effectively pinned down. Sooner of later the rifleman would hit his target, Fargo knew. And he knew one thing more: the gunman was Hobbs. Somehow, the man had crawled away, tortured and pain-racked as he was, and survived. He had survived, but he was forever maimed, probably still wearing every scar that Assiniboin had given him. He had survived and hidden out, perhaps even returned to the cabin, and had watched and waited. He'd found himself a high place that let him see the land in all directions and waited. He was a twisted, sick monster from the start. Now he was an obsessed, twisted monster, living only for revenge.

Another rifle shot hit the edge of the wagon wheel to break off his thoughts, and Fargo glanced at Robin. Her eyes told him she knew who had them pinned down. He called to her, his voice a low growl. "We can't stay here," he said, and she nodded. His glance went to the line of oak not far in back of the wagon, then to the sky. There was no more than another few hours of daylight left. "I'm going to try to get behind the horses. I'll draw his fire. Soon as I start, you get up and come after me," he said, and she nodded.

He half-rose onto one knee, dug his right foot hard into the ground, gathered himself, and pushed off with all his strength. The distance was but a few scant feet and he counted on surprise, Hobbs using up precious seconds to react. Fargo raced forward, for a few moments into the clear space between the wagon and the brace of horses. The first rifle shot missed by a good margin, the second came closer, but Fargo had reached the horses. He continued to race forward, past the horses' heads, into the open again for a few seconds. He skidded to a halt in the clear and knew Hobbs was swinging his rifle around to fire again. Fargo risked another precious split second before he dived back behind the horses and the shot grazed the back of his head.

But he saw Robin behind the horses, one hand against the left shaft as she gasped in deep breaths of air. He came to her, took the nearest horse by the cheek strap, and began to lead the animal slowly forward. "Stay right where you are behind the horses," he called over his shoulder as he moved at a long angle toward the trees.

Hobbs fired two pairs of shots that bracketed the horses, but Fargo held the frightened animals from bolting as he pulled back on the cheek strap. He stroked the horse, murmuring soothingly, keeping his voice calm as he kept the animals moving slowly toward the tree line. Four more shots split the air, two hitting the Owensboro. Fired in angry frustration, Fargo was certain.

As they reached the oak, he found a place large enough to let the wagon slide in as two more shots slammed into the trees near the tailgate. He pulled Robin into the trees as he peered across to the hawthorn. The figure stepped into sight for a brief moment and Fargo saw the wide-brimmed stetson pulled low and the full-length tan horseman's duster, a figure that seemed more an apparition than real, faceless and bodyless. Hobbs quickly stepped back into the hawthorns.

"He can't come at us now, not across the open ground," Fargo said. "He'll have to wait till dark."

"And we just stay and wait?" Robin asked.

"No choice. We can't go into the open, either," Fargo said. "The night will give us the advantage."

"How?" Robin frowned. "It seems to me it'll give him the same advantage. We won't know where he is, but he'll know where we are."

"That's right," Fargo said, and she frowned back. "Which means we'll have to change that when the time comes."

"How?"

"I'm working on that," Fargo said, and sat down against a thick oak where he could see across the open land.

Robin settled down close beside him. "What if we hadn't come back? What if we'd gone on into the north country? Would he still have waited the entire winter?" she asked.

"Maybe. He's a madman now, a different kind than he was before. He's obsessed. Revenge is all he has left to live for," Fargo said. "But he knew that wouldn't happen. He knew all he had to do was wait."

She shivered against him. He put one arm around her and she grew quiet. Together, they watched the day begin to fade and dusk roll across the hills. Fargo rose and pulled himself onto the wagon. Hobbs could see the bulk of the big Owensboro in the trees but little else, he knew. He beckoned Robin into the wagon and pulled a crate across the floorboards behind the driver's seat. "When the time comes, you're going to drive out into the open hell-bent-for-leather," he said. "But you'll be driving from here inside the wagon."

Robin shook her head. "The reins aren't long enough to reach back here."

Fargo frowned, reached out to take hold of the end of the reins, and realized that she was absolutely right. They had to be three feet longer. "Be right back," he said, and carefully swung from the wagon. He strode to the Ovaro, cut a length of lariat, and returned to the wagon with it, where he tied a piece of the rope to each of the reins. "They are now," he said, and handed Robin the ropes that extended the reins three feet.

She grasped them, tested them, and nodded.

"When you roll, he's going to fire off at least three shots at the driver's seat before he realizes you're not there. You'll be low in here. Any shots he fires into the canvas will likely go over your head or go wild altogether."

"Likely?" she echoed.

"No guarantees, honey," he grunted, and saw the dusk begin to fade into darkness. "You stay right here," he said as he swung from the wagon again. This time he returned carrying the big Sharps and he halted outside the canvas and spoke to Robin. "You hear me?" he asked.

"Yes."

"When I yell, you go charging out," he said. "And keep your head down. All you have to do is keep those horses running hard."

"How far?"

"You keep going. Don't stop and don't look back," he said. "If it goes right, I'll catch up to you."

"And if it doesn't?"

"You'll be on your way. Chances are he won't go after you," Fargo said. "It's my head he wants.

162

That'll satisfy him." He left the side of the wagon and hurried through the trees to halt some dozen yards back.

The moon hadn't come out high enough yet and the open land was a stretch of blackness against the deeper black of the hawthorns beyond. Fargo dropped to one knee, the rifle at his shoulder, though he didn't sight along it yet. Hobbs would be careful. He might well crawl his way across the open land, not unlike a viper seeking its prey in the darkness. He was probably doing just that, Fargo decided, and he allowed another five minutes to pass.

It was a calculated decision. If he were wrong, Hobbs would be too close already. But Fargo's night vision had been tested many times and he saw nothing move across the open land. He counted off another minute and lifted his voice in a hoarse, rasping sound. "Now," he said, and heard the snap of the reins across the horses' backs. The wagon rolled into the clear, moving fast in but a few seconds as Robin snapped the reins again. But Fargo's eyes were sweeping the open land and he was ready as the shots exploded. Three of them, aimed at the driver's seat of the wagon. He had the big Sharps aimed as the third flash cut into the darkness.

He fired, just behind the flash, behind it again, to the left and the right and in front of it, and he heard the sharp cry of pain before the rifle was emptied. He stayed, waited, and began to move forward in a zigzag crouch just as the moon rose to cast its pale light over the open land. He saw the dark form on the grass and veered toward it. When he saw it move, he dived to one side as the rifle shot hurtled past him. He hit the ground, rolled, came up with the Colt in his hand and firing. He poured four shots into the dark shape before he realized it wasn't moving. He rose, more carefully this time, and moved toward it again.

The shape made no movement and Fargo had the Colt poised to fire as he reached the figure. Walter Hobbs lay half on his back, his lower body twisted one way, his torso the other, and the rifle on the ground alongside him. The wide-brimmed stetson had fallen from his head. The few tufts of hair were a reminder of the Assiniboin's art of cruelty. Fargo saw that his shots had struck Hobbs in the head and the body, red stains widening on the long horseman's duster. Judas had paid the price once and for all. The long duster could be his shroud, Fargo grunted as he turned away, picked up the Sharps, and walked back to the Ovaro.

He climbed onto the horse and caught up to the wagon, which seemed to race through the night without a driver. "Whoa," he called out, and Robin brought the brace of horses to a halt. He swung onto the driver's seat as she half-leapt out of the wagon, her arms around him, her lips pressed hard against his. He felt the wetness of her cheeks and rubbed his hand across them. "You always cry when you drive?" He smiled.

"Only when I'm praying at the same time," she said, and pulled him to her again. "Take the long way back, Fargo. Please?"

"I was thinking the same thing," he said as her soft warm breasts pressed into his chest. There were different ways to forget. This would be one of the best.

LOOKING FORWARD!

**The following is the opening
section from the next novel in the exciting
Trailsman series from Signet:**

THE TRAILSMAN #113
SOUTHERN BELLES

*Summer, 1860, on the Mississippi River,
where muddy waters conceal dark deeds
and shady schemes, and where death
lurks just below the surface . . .*

The big man astride the magnificent black-and-
white pinto followed the west bank of a canyon
stream in Montana Territory, deep inside Sioux
country. Although aware that friction existed
between the Indians and bluecoats at Fort Laramie,
far to the south, he rode easy in the saddle; the Sioux
were his friends, the troopers as white of skin as he.

General Scott McRae, a man he'd never met,
had dispatched twenty-five troopers with orders to
punish the seven bands of Lakota Sioux roaming
west of the Black Hills. General McRae was convinced one of the bands had attacked a wagon train
of settlers and massacred them all. The remains of
the wagons and settlers had been found within
Lakota territory, ill-defined as it was.

The survivors of a Two Kettle *tiospaye* had told
the Trailsman all of this information two days ago.

They also mentioned being shelled by a big gun—the "iron giant on wheels," one had called the cannon.

"The bluecoats struck without warning early in the morning," the wounded warrior told Fargo. "Our women were building cooking fires outside the tepees when the iron giant roared. The ground beneath my belly bounced and shook. The women screamed. They ran inside their tepees to hide. Then the bluecoats attacked us. They shot many people, Trailsman—women, children, and old, helpless elders. Some butchered us with their long knives while others burned our tepees. The ten of us you see played like we were dead. Between us we know enough of the white man's words to piece together what their leader said to his soldiers. The General McRae does a bad thing. We Lakota didn't bother those wagons. Neither did we kill any of the *wasicun*. War Chief Pony-Runs-Long did it. I speak the truth, Trailsman."

Skye Fargo knew the Cheyenne war chief. Pony-Runs-Long was insane and reckless, but bold at best. He had vowed never to make peace with the Great Father in Washington. For years the cavalry had been chasing him and his warriors, but the cunning war chief gave them the slip every time the troopers got close. Now it appeared Pony-Runs-Long had done it again, and shifted the blame onto the Lakota, his natural enemy.

Fargo moved up the canyon slowly, scanning through the green canopy of whispering pine, cottonwood, and weeping willow at the jagged, wind-blown crests of the sheer rocky walls on either side of him. He paused when he rode into a clear spot and took a closer look. He knew Sans Arc were in the canyon. Maybe warriors on the ridges would see him. If any were up there, they didn't reveal their presence to him. Fargo rode on.

He'd gone less than a hundred yards when muted echoes of cannon and rifle fire reverberated off the canyon walls. The sounds came from far up the canyon. Fargo nudged the Ovaro into a gallop. There was no need for a faster pace; the detachment of soldiers would finish their work and be gone by the time he got there.

Rounding a bend, he smelled smoke. Riding farther, he saw wisps of smoke hanging low over the stream and among lower branches of trees. All the gunfire had ceased. In the far distance he heard women wailing, and he quickened the powerful stallion's gait. The smoke became increasingly pronounced the closer he got to the encampment. Then he saw it, or what was left of it.

The encampment stood in an opening among the pine trees over on the east bank near the mouth of the canyon. Beyond that opening stretched a prairie where buffalo herds—the Lakota people's main source of food—roamed, grazing at leisure. On that prairie rode the column of troopers, mere specks now. The iron giant rolled at the rear of the column.

Fargo reined the Ovaro toward the burning tepees. None had their covering intact. The buffalo hides so carefully tanned by the women—it took a minimum of twelve—and painstakingly sewn together with threads of sinew lay smoldering on the ground around the tepee poles. Several tepees had been demolished in an instant by cannon balls. The people's meager possessions were scattered everywhere: colorful shields—most with eagle feathers attached; water bags made from buffalo stomachs; gourd dippers; cradle boards, several with hoods that still smoldered; and buffalo robes by the dozens. Black Cheyenne or Crow scalps fluttered in the updraft of tepee poles still standing and aflame.

Half-naked warriors lay where they had been gunned down or met death by a flashing saber. Crumpled bodies of women—some still carrying their babies—lay where they were caught while fleeing the soldiers. A baby with a bleeding head wound sat crying between its mother's outstretched, lifeless arms. An old man stood on wobbly legs, watching the tepee poles burn. He seemed confused by it all, as though he couldn't believe what had happened, as though he could blink and make it be as before.

Four wounded warriors staggered to the old man as Fargo rode up and reined the pinto to a halt. He dismounted and went to the crying infant first. Blood from a gash in the naked girl's forehead streamed over her eyes and down her face. Fargo believed she would survive, albeit with an ugly scar that in later life she could point to and tell the little ones gathered round her about the day the bluecoats had come. He removed his neckerchief and wiped the blood from the little girl's eyes and face, then tied the neckerchief around her head to stop the flow of blood. He hefted her in his arms and carried her to the warriors and old man.

Handing the child to the warrior least wounded— like the old man the brave was in shock more than anything else, although he bled from a saber wound on his left thigh—Fargo turned his attention to the warrior's companions. All three had multiple rifle or pistol wounds, one so bad that Fargo couldn't imagine what was holding the man together. Speaking in the Lakota dialect, Fargo told the dazed warriors, "Sit and let me have a look at your wounds."

The warrior shook his head, then fell dead, leaking blood from six holes in his body.

Fargo moved to the next man. He had been shot in the right shoulder and creased by a bullet on the left upper arm. The bullet that hit his shoulder had gone clear through. The young warrior appeared healthy enough to make Fargo reckon he would live. The warrior had scars above both nipples, attesting that he was a sun-dancer. As such, the crease on his arm meant nothing. Fargo told him, "Find some fresh sage. Strip off the tender leaves and roll them into two balls, then pack one where the bullet went in, the other where it came out."

The warrior nodded and walked away.

As Fargo stepped to the next man, six warriors rode in from the mouth of the canyon. Sliding off their ponies, they looked questioningly at the big white man, as though he was responsible for the death and destruction they saw. It was a tense moment when Fargo withdrew his Colt and handed it to one of them to show he had come in peace.

The warrior promptly returned the weapon to him and grunted, "We saw bluecoats riding away on the prairie. We know you couldn't do this alone. But you could have helped the bluecoats. Why are you here, *wasicun*? To make sure all our relatives died?"

Before Fargo could answer, the old man muttered dryly, "Be quiet, Chases Bears, before your tongue shames you. The white man came after the bluecoats killed everybody. He had nothing to do with what your eyes see. Now, *wasicun*, you can speak. Tell us why you are here."

Fargo proceeded to wipe blood from the back left-shoulder gunshot wound of the warrior he had stepped to. The slug had ripped open a long gash on the warrior's back, but not penetrated his body. The warrior was in no danger of an early death. Fargo answered, "I came to warn my Sans Arc brothers and sisters that the cavalry was looking for them, to hurt them, for something bad the Cheyenne did."

"Unh," the old man grunted. He swept a hand in a wide, flat arc and went on, "Then the Cheyenne, they are the cause of all this?"

"Yes," Fargo began. "Pony-Runs-Long attacked a wagon train in Wyoming Territory. All the settlers were massacred. Bluecoats from Fort Laramie found them. Because it happened in the Lakota peoples' hunting territory they—"

Chases Bears interrupted. He spat angrily, then spoke. "Enough. We know Pony-Runs-Long. He has been causing trouble for me and my brothers a long time." Turning to the old man, Chases Bears said tenderly, "Sit in shade, *tunkasila* Two Eagles. We will take care of everything."

"No," the grandfather replied. "It is my duty to help. There are many people to be buried. Raise a big scaffold. We will send them to the spirit world in the Lakota way. Find my pipe."

Chases Bears and the other five nonwounded warriors walked away to obey Grandfather Two Eagles. Fargo tended to the third warrior's wounds, two pistol shots, both in his lower neck, both fired at extremely close range. Both bullets had missed arteries, the only reason why the warrior still lived. The weakened man was in no condition to help the burial party. Fargo suggested he too pack his wounds with sage then sit in the shade.

Though the warrior complied with Fargo's first suggestion, he did not accept the second. He helped his brothers build the scaffold. Fargo did, too. Two

Eagles oversaw its construction at the site he selected on top of the east wall of the canyon, where it dropped off and met the prairie.

In Fargo's opinion it was truly a remarkable feat. Not only was it required to them to fell the many lodgepole pine to support the huge scaffold, then lug them up to the crest and construct the lattice-shaped platform on which the dead would be laid to rest, they also had to carry the dead up to the scaffold. Not a small chore for seven able-bodied men and three walking-wounded.

As the dead were brought to the scaffold, the three women cut a bit of hair from each or snipped off fingernails or toenails. Fargo watched them put the trimmings on a large piece of buckskin spread on the ground under the platform. The pile of hair and nail clippings grew larger and larger. He knew that after the burial ceremony the buckskin and cuttings would be tied into a bundle and kept in a secret place for one year, at which time the bundle would be buried, thereby releasing the souls of the dead. In the meantime a similar bundle would be prepared. It would be hidden, too—but not as secretly as the first bundle. There were those—such as the Cheyenne and Crow—who would dearly love to find the bundle, open it, and scatter the trimmings in the four winds, thereby releasing the souls prematurely and causing them to wander forever and not enter the spirit world. It was serious business. Fargo respected it.

Fargo counted thirty-two bodies as they were passed up to him and Chases Bears to arrange on the platform. A full moon hung high in the starlit sky before they put the last lifeless form on the platform.

They dropped to the ground and joined the others already sitting in a circle around a small fire.

Fargo watched Two Eagles fill two halves of semi-large geodes with a mixture of flat cedar, sweet-grass, and crumbled sage, the Sioux people's sacred incense ingredients, then drop a small, glowing ember into each. The old man took one of the smoldering geodes under the scaffold platform and held it high as he walked back and forth beneath the bodies. In this way all were purified by the smoke from the incense. Finished, he set the geode on the ground beneath the platform and left it there to smolder out.

Then he brought the other geode with him when he returned to the circle of men and women, who sat facing a small fire in its center. Between his position on the eastern rim of the circle lay the open buckskin of trimmings and his pipe bag, both resting on an east-to-west axis cutting through his position and the fire. The buckskin was nearest to the fire, the pipe bag within easy reach when he sat.

Two Eagles held the smoldering geode close to the buckskin and washed it and the trimmings thoroughly with the incense smoke. Finally he set the geode on the ground in front of his pipe bag, stepped to his position in the circle, and sat on his haunches, facing the fire.

Fargo, the warriors, and the women sat and remained silent as Two Eagles began the sacred rite, Releasing of the Soul. He rubbed sage on both his palms, then handed the sage to the warrior sitting to his left, who did the same, then passed it to the warrior sitting on his left. The ball of sage moved sunwise around the circle so each person could purify his hands before receiving the sacred pipe.

The pipe bag before him was liberally adorned with porcupine quills, tiny beads of all colors, and the opening tied with a length of thong fashioned out of buckskin. Secured to the thong was Two

Eagles' *cungleska*, a small medicine wheel backed by a hard-to-come-by, hence treasured, piece of shiny seashell shaped to conform with the circular medicine wheel. Tied to the sacred hoop were the two eagle trail feathers Two Eagles had received during his naming ceremony. They were misshapen now, the tips curled, some of the individual feathers constituting the whole missing altogether.

Fargo knew the old man revered the *cungleska* and feathers; they were the old man's bond that connected him to the past, present, and future.

Slowly, reverently, Two Eagles removed the *cungleska* and feathers, then opened the pipe bag. He took out the bowl and long stem of his pipe. He moved both parts back and forth in the smoke rising from the geode to purify each. Fargo watched him firmly but gently connect the bowl and stem, then pass the whole pipe through the smoke. Then the old man opened his tobacco pouch, removed a pinch of the sacred *cincasa*, and offered it to the spirit in the west.

The warriors and Fargo began singing the pipe-filling song, which continued while the old man made similar offerings to the spirits in the north, east, south, to his Maka Ina, Mother Earth, which he held to the ground, to Wanka Tanka, the Great Spirit, which he held skyward. The seventh pinch was for the spotted eagle who would carry his and their later prayers aloft and release them into the universe.

The old man stood, faced west, pointed the pipe's stem in that direction, and offered the first of six prayers, which he repeated when facing the spirits in the other three directions and looking down at Mother Earth and looking up when praying to the Great Spirit. "O Wanka Tanka, Two Eagles is praying to you. Hear me, Wanka Tanka. I am praying for you to take the souls of my dead relatives across the great waters, there to be among their ancestors who live in peace with all human beings' souls, even the *wasicuns*'. O Wanka Tanka, forgive the bluecoats for what they did this day, for they know not the truth. In your own way punish those who were responsible. They are crazy, Wanka Tanka, and must be stopped from causing trouble. *Me-tock-we-ah-see.*" Having said the Lakota equivalent of amen, Two Eagles sat and lit his pipe with the burning end of a twig taken from the fire.

After taking a few draws and exhaling the smoke, he started the pipe around the circle. When it came back to him, he smoked it out, disassembled the two parts, and returned them to the pipe bag. He said, "*Me-tock-we-ah-see.*" The ceremony was over.

The women wrapped and tied the buckskin bundle. Fargo and the warriors followed Two Eagles down to the destroyed *tiospaye*. When they got there, Chases Bears turned to face Fargo and asked, "Where will you go?"

"I'm looking for a white woman. She was taken from a wagon train passing through or near your lands. All I know is she was taken by Indians. Which tribe or band is unknown."

One of the other warriors spoke up. "Chases Bears, I know of such a white woman."

"Then, tell us, Crying Fox," Chases Bears insisted.

"By all means, do," Fargo added.

"The Miniconju have her," Crying Fox began. "They captured her during a night raid to steal Cheyenne women from Pony-Runs-Long's camp. Hoksila told me they were surprised to see a white face among the Cheyenne faces when they got back to their encampment."

"She's well, I hope?" Fargo inquired. "Did you see her? Describe her to me."

"No, I didn't see her. Hoksila's hunting party and the one I was in met on the prairie one morning. He told me about the raid and stealing the white woman by mistake."

"How long ago was that?" Fargo pressed.

"During the new moon before the last full moon. Raids to steal women and ponies always happen when the night sky is good and dark."

About thirty-eight or so days ago, Fargo thought. "When did your hunting party bump into Hoksila's?" Fargo asked.

"Ten moons ago," Crying Fox replied.

"Did Hoksila mention what the Miniconju did with her?"

"Hoksila said none of the warriors wanted her. He said they gave her to an old Miniconju woman who could no longer gather wood."

"Crying Fox, will you take me to Hoksila?"

"For what you have done this day, yes, I will take you to my brothers, the Miniconju."

The three women walked up carrying two identical bundles. Fargo noticed one bundle had been double-tied. He didn't know whether it or the other one held the souls of the dead Sans Arcs. Nobody other than the three women would ever know, and they would die before revealing the truth. All three women had shorn their hair. Though they looked funny, Fargo didn't so much as grin. They would be in mourning for one full year. Two of them had also cut off the tips of their noses, a sure sign that they were now widows. They made themselves ugly on purpose, so no man would have them, so all who saw them would know they were grieving widows. It was the custom, a show of respect for their departed husbands.

The young woman with a whole nose took the baby girl from the wounded warrior.

Fargo said, "Well, Crying Fox, there is nothing more for us to do here. If we ride hard and fast maybe we will find your Miniconju brothers before the army does."

They shook hands all around, then Fargo and Crying Fox mounted up. The warriors, women, and old man watched them ride out of the canyon and disappear on the grassy prairie.

Fargo headed north, into the great unknown.